T0193511

SUDDENLY
IT WAS
THE LAST DAY
OF MY LIFE

I THOUGHT
I HAD
MORE TIME

MICHAEL J. WAGGONER

WESTBOW
PRESS®
A DIVISION OF THOMAS NELSON
& ZONDERVAN

WestBow Press books may be ordered through booksellers or by contacting:

WestBow Press
A Division of Thomas Nelson & Zondervan
1663 Liberty Drive
Bloomington, IN 47403
www.westbowpress.com
844-714-3454

ISBN: 978-1-6642-9514-8 (sc)
ISBN: 978-1-6642-9515-5 (hc)
ISBN: 978-1-6642-9513-1 (e)

Library of Congress Control Number: 2023904716

Print information available on the last page.

WestBow Press rev. date: 03/29/2023

When I initially started writing this book, it was my intention to write it for my children and grandchildren. I wanted to share some of the things I felt were important about life. And indeed, it is to them that I dedicate this book.

But as I wrote the book, I came to realize I was really writing it for myself. I was forced to truly look at my life, how I had lived it and how I should live it going forward.

It is my hope that if others should read it, they would come to the same conclusions I did. Therefore, I also dedicate this book to any who should read it and whose lives are enriched in any meaningful way, no matter how small. May they be truly blessed.

And inasmuch as it is appointed unto men once to die, and after this *cometh* judgment.

—Hebrews 9:27 (ASV)

ACKNOWLEDGMENTS

I would like to thank God, who gave me the time, health and resources to write this novel. As I told Him on many occasions, if I'm not writing for His glory, then I'm wasting my time.

I want to thank my beautiful wife, Monica, for her support and helpful suggestions and encouragement. Thank you, my love. I could not have done it without you.

I also want to thank my father-in-law, Richard D. Gordon, and my high school English teacher, Pat Jackson, for the invaluable help and insights they gave me. You both showed me things I would not have seen on my own. Thank you so much.

CHAPTER 1

THE END

> What is your life? You are a mist that appears for a little while and then vanishes.
>
> —James 4:14 (NIV)

I had not expected to die today.

When I woke up on this frosty fall morning, dying was the last thing on my mind. In fact, it wasn't on my mind at all. I had slept in fits and starts and was still tired and groggy as I pulled myself out of bed and got dressed. I suffered from sleep apnea and nowadays basically felt tired all the time. It had become part of my way of life.

I was in a hurry, as usual. I had to go to the city to see my son Keith, run a few errands and keep an appointment. I hated being late.

I was thinking about a lot of things as I went through my morning routine. My mind was troubled about Keith, who was experiencing a lot of difficulties in his teen years. He was my youngest and was struggling to stay in school.

He had sent me a text, which I read as soon as I got up. *Dad, can you send me forty dollars for vapes?* He texted.

Sure, I texted back. I really didn't want to spend the forty dollars for vapes, but I knew that if I refused or delayed, he might get angry and not go to school. He had difficulties controlling his anger due to fetal alcohol syndrome, and the smallest perceived slight could trigger him. I had learned through hard experience not to push him, so I sent the money.

There was a voicemail on my phone from my job asking me to work a twelve-hour shift tomorrow instead of my usual eight. I was tired. I was run down. I was in my fifties, and all I wanted to do was retire. Life had become a grind, and I felt like I was on a treadmill going nowhere. I really did not want to work overtime, but I wanted the money, so I phoned them back and told them I'd do it.

As I struggled to get my socks on, something that I was finding more and more difficult to do as I gained weight and became less flexible, my wife Julie woke up.

"Johnny honey," she said, "before you go, can you go to the drugstore and buy that medication I was telling you about for the elderly lady at church? She really needs it today."

I didn't have a lot of extra time if I wanted to get to that appointment on time. "I'm kind of in a hurry," I said.

She rolled over and pulled her covers up onto her head. "You always are."

A pang of guilt ran through me. She was right. I was always in a hurry. It seemed that my entire life was composed of just running from one thing to the next. I didn't even have time to pick up some medication for an elderly widow.

"All right, I'll do it," I said. "I should have just enough time."

"Thanks, love. Bring it back here, and I'll take it over to her after I get up."

I got into my newer-model SUV and drove to the pharmacy, which luckily was already open. It had snowed overnight, and the road was slick in places. This was just wonderful, I thought. Now my trip to the city would take even longer.

When I got home, I gave my wife the medication and kissed her goodbye. "I should be about five hours or so," I said, not realizing it would be the last time I would ever kiss her beautiful face.

"Have a good day, love."

"I hope so," I replied, but I didn't have any real confidence that I would.

The appointment was about Keith's school performance, which wasn't going well. I was busy—too busy to relax and feel good about things. I was working a full-time job, running a business with my uncle, still helping out my kids and looking after my wife, who wasn't always in the best of health. Something was always coming up. My kids were often at odds with each other, and with my wife and me, and it seemed I was continuously just trying to hold everything together. Good days were few and far between.

I pulled out on to the highway and began my journey. I felt rushed. With the traffic and the temperature increase, I reasoned that the snow would probably be almost gone from the pavement, and it was, at least for the first ten minutes or so. But then ice patches began to appear. I slowed down and put my car into four-wheel drive. I looked at the clock. I reckoned that if I could just drive the speed limit, I could make that appointment on time. Of course, driving the speed limit was not my normal practice. I usually drove much faster. Driving slowly was not in my nature.

My daughter Naomi phoned me on my cell phone. "Your grandson wants to know if he can talk to you," she said.

"Sure. Put him on."

"Hi, Grandpa," Tyler said joyfully. "Could you play checkers with me tomorrow?"

I hesitated. I hated saying no to my grandson. I had been teaching him how to play checkers, and we were both really enjoying it.

"I'm sorry Tyler," I finally said, "but Grandpa has to work overtime tomorrow. We'll have to do it another time."

"Oh, OK," he said with obvious disappointment in his voice.

After a short conversation with Naomi, I hung up. I treasured the time I spent with my grandson. It just seemed it didn't happen enough; I was always too busy.

I prayed a bit as I continued driving. I had been a believer for most of my life, but I hadn't always been totally dedicated. Other things would often crowd out the spiritual.

As I merged on to the freeway, I noticed a huge pothole right where the exit ramp met the highway. I definitely did not want to hit that with my nice SUV; too much damage might occur. So I swerved left to miss it as I entered the freeway. I didn't shoulder check. That was a big mistake.

The warning bell beeped but it was too late. At that instant, a large tractor trailer was barrelling past. He was focused on his radio and didn't see me swerve into his lane. We collided. I briefly heard the loud shrieking of metal and felt an intense pain. Then everything went black. There was no more pain, just complete darkness.

For me it was all over. My journey on this earth had ended.

CHAPTER 2

THE TRANSITION

And the dust returns to the ground it came from, and the
spirit returns to God who gave it.
                                    —Ecclesiastes 12:7 (NIV)

Except it hadn't. My journey was about to continue.

I felt myself rising out of the car right up through the roof until I was twenty feet or so above the accident scene. I saw the truck that had hit me. It had skidded to a stop a few hundred meters away. The driver was emerging from the cab. He appeared unharmed, but he was clearly shaken up. He frantically raced toward my car while dialling 911 on his phone.

I felt completely free. I had no pain. I seemed to be the same person I'd been just moments earlier when I'd swerved to avoid the pothole. Nothing seemed to be different except that I wasn't in my body any longer, and I was floating a few feet above the accident scene.

I looked at my SUV. It was a crumpled mess. So much for avoiding damage by swerving to miss a pothole. I could see a body through the windshield. Was that me? I looked dead. In fact, I was quite certain I was dead. I stared at the corpse. I had never seen myself in 3D before. Was that what I actually looked like to others? I had difficulty believing it was me. But it was me all right; I could not deny it. My body, the body of Johnny Donaldson, was scrunched up within the wreckage and covered in blood. There was no way anybody could survive that.

At that moment I felt another presence beside me. I looked and saw the most beautiful creature looking down on the accident scene with me. He had wings, and he looked at me with affection. I gasped when I saw him.

"I am your guardian angel," he said. "I have been with you your entire life, watching over you. Today I was instructed to not intervene."

I was speechless. Was this real or just a dream? I had heard of guardian angels, but I had never really given them much thought. I'd certainly never thought I'd had one with me for my entire life.

I finally spoke. "So this is really happening? This is not a bad dream? I really am dead?"

He paused for a moment before replying. "Yes, this is real. You died in that car accident a few moments ago, and your soul left your body. Your body is dead. It will be resurrected one day and reunited with your soul, but for now it will return to its original state. Now, your soul, which has taken on your bodily form, will live on in the afterlife, as you humans like to call it. It isn't really an afterlife; it is the real life that you will live for eternally."

"The only question is where you will be living it."

I thought about that last sentence. I wasn't sure I was ready for the answer. We stayed and watched as the emergency vehicles arrived and took my corpse away. There were no sirens as they left. There was no need to hurry for a dead person.

My angel spoke again. "Because you did not expect to die today, you do not have to move on as yet. The Lord has allowed you to stay for a time, if you so wish. When you have decided that you're ready to move on, let me know."

"Move on?" I asked. "Move on to where?"

"You will be taken to the place where you will spend your eternal life. But first that will have to be determined."

I certainly didn't feel like I was ready to move on—in fact, I didn't like the idea of being dead. I wasn't ready to be dead yet. There were too many things I still needed to do in my life. This was too soon.

"I want to live again," I said. "I'm not ready to be dead yet. Can I go back into my body?"

"No, you cannot," he replied. "I was instructed to not intervene. You cannot go back."

I didn't like his answer, but it looked as if I had no choice. I paused and thought for a few moments. As I did, I looked more closely at the angel.

His presence was awe-inspiring. He wore a bright blue tunic, and his hair was golden and curly. His wings flapped gently behind him. He seemed completely in his element as he hovered in the air above the accident scene. To think that he had always been near me for my entire life was astonishing to me. He had always been there, but I could not see him, and I had not even been aware of his existence.

"I will stay for a while," I finally said. "I want to see my family."

"All right," he replied. "That will be fine. Where to first?"

"I want to see my son Keith, who I was going to see this morning after my appointment."

"Follow me," he said, and we began to fly.

We lifted higher over the landscape and began to soar. I went slowly at first, but I soon learned to pick up speed. It seemed that I knew how to fly instinctively. It was exhilarating.

"I used to have dreams about doing this," I said to my angel.

"Perhaps those dreams were preparing you. Dreams are sometimes used for that purpose. They often have more meaning attached to them than humans realize."

It seemed so effortless. We reached my youngest son's home in what seemed like seconds. He lived with his mother, my ex-wife Lindsey.

As we entered the dwelling, I saw her sitting in a recliner reading her phone. She seemed totally at ease and completely unaware that we were there. I went over and stood directly in front of her. She didn't move. I waved my hand in front of her face. There was no response. She had no idea we were there.

My angel seemed amused.

"Can I communicate with her?" I asked.

"No. Permission has not been granted."

I had never believed in ghosts or spirits in my lifetime. Now I was one. As I looked at her, I wondered if she would even shed a tear when she learned of my death. We had not had the best of relationships, and I knew that she blamed me for wrecking her life. We shared custody of Keith, which kept us in contact over the years. Our relationship was, for the most part, civil. One thing I knew was that she was going to miss the child-support payments I paid her every month.

We moved into my son's room. He was not in a good mood. He was arguing with his girlfriend on the phone.

"I was just talking to him," she said, "that's all it was. Nothing more than that."

Keith let out a string of profanities. "Yeah, well, the next time I see him I'm going to kill him," he said, followed by more expletives.

Anger poured out of him. He hung up on her and began punching things. He punched his bed. He punched the wall. I just wanted to hug him and let him know it would be all right.

"Can I touch him?" I asked my angel.

"You can, but he won't know that you did it."

I put my hand on his shoulder. Then I wrapped my arm around him. He didn't notice me at all. It was as if I wasn't even there.

He went into the room where Lindsey was sitting. "I'm not going to school today. If I go, I'm going to murder somebody," Keith said to her.

"Well, then it's probably better if you don't go," his mother replied.

"Dad is coming to see me later."

Of course I wouldn't be. Not alive, anyway. A great sadness came over me as I realized I would never be able to talk to him again. I was in a different dimension now. I could see and hear him just as well, if not better, than when I was in my body. But I could not communicate with him. I didn't want to leave; I wanted to talk to my son. I wanted to tell him I loved him and that I always would even after I died.

I tried. "I love you, son. It's going to be all right. It'll be fine."

He didn't look at me or respond in any way. I continued to watch him, but there was seemingly nothing I could do for him.

After a few minutes I turned to my angel. "I guess we might as well go. I want to see my wife and other children."

We left and flew to the town where my home was. This time I led the way. I seemed to have no problem knowing how to get there. It seemed to take only minutes to cover the hundred- kilometre distance.

As we entered the town, we flew directly over my uncle's house. He was outside and climbing into his truck. We had run a business together for the past twenty-five years. We too had had a rocky relationship at times but had managed to stay in partnership over the years. I didn't know what would happen to the business now that I would no longer be there. Would he even be able to keep it going? He seemed to be calmly going about his routine. Apparently, he had not yet heard about my death.

We moved on. As we approached my home, I saw that our respite worker, Fred, was picking up my disabled son Stephen for the day. It was not going well. My son was refusing to get into the van.

Fred was talking to him politely, but Stephen was not budging. "You need to get in," he said, "We have a lot of things to do today that you will like."

My son was having none of it. He just stood there with his arms crossed and a sullen look on his face. "I'm not going to get in if I'm not allowed to bring my CD."

"Well, your mom said you couldn't bring it. Maybe you can bring it tomorrow," Fred offered.

Stephen continued to stonewall.

Fred then brought out his nuclear weapon. "You don't want me to phone your dad, do you? Because if you don't get in, I will phone him."

That got a response. My son knew that would not go well for him. I had been the one person who could discipline him and get him to do the things he needed to do. He wasn't fond of my techniques.

"Don't you phone my dad," he snapped as he opened the door to the van and got in.

It was surreal to watch. I was now observing in real time events that went on every day without my being present. I now knew what it was like to be invisible. If it weren't for the fact that I was dead, I might have enjoyed it.

We moved on to the house. I paused. "I don't know if I can do this," I said to the angel. "I told her I'd be back in five hours. I kissed her but didn't tell her I loved her. She isn't going to take the news of my death very well. I don't know if I can bear to watch."

My angel did not respond immediately. He gave me time, and then he spoke. "It's your decision. God has granted you more time on the earth, if you wish. But you may also move on at any time you desire. I cannot advise you on what you should do."

I thought about what he said. I knew the right thing was to see my wife. I knew it was going to be difficult. She was going to be an emotional mess, but perhaps I could comfort her in some way.

"Let's go in," I said.

And with that, we passed through the wall into my house.

CHAPTER 3

MINISTERING SPIRITS

For He will command His angels concerning you to guard
you in all your ways. They will lift you up in their hands,
so that you will not strike your foot against a stone.
—Psalm 91:11–12 (NIV)

My wife was calm. She had not yet received the news of my death. She was
preparing some food in the kitchen.

I wanted to talk to her but was unable. Something prevented me. I
jumped up and down right in front of her, but she didn't notice. She had
no idea I was there. I wanted to communicate with her in some way but
didn't know how. How could I make my presence known?

"You cannot speak to or appear to her," my angel said.

I looked around. I saw a photo of us together on the refrigerator door.
It was always in the same spot. It had been taken the day we renewed our
marriage vows. *Maybe,* I thought, *I can move it somewhere where she'll see
it and will know it was me.*

I went over to the fridge door and reached for the photo. My hand
went right through it. It didn't move.

"That would be a kind gesture," my angel said. "Focus all of your
energy on it. You should be able to move it."

I did as he suggested. It took great concentration and focus, but as I
touched the photo again it began to move—ever so slowly at first and then
faster. After a great effort I was finally able to dislodge it from the fridge
magnet and it fell to the floor. I tried to pick it up but couldn't.

My wife didn't notice it. She was busy at the stove cutting up vegetables for a pot of soup. She had her earplugs in and was listening to something as she worked.

I continued to observe her. "I'm right here! Can't you see me? Can't you hear me?" I yelled as loudly as I could.

There was not the slightest response.

She had no idea I was there or that I was even dead. I wanted to talk to her. I wanted to tell her what had happened. I wanted to tell her that I loved her and that everything would be all right. But she was completely oblivious.

It was such an irony. All those years she had complained that I wasn't listening to her and now I was right beside her shouting as loud as I could, and she completely ignored me! I attempted to touch her. She didn't notice. There was no flinch—not a gesture, not a single movement.

Then the doorbell rang. It was the police. The two officers asked my wife who she was and if they could come in.

Once inside, they asked her to sit. She was startled. They calmly and professionally told her that I had been killed in a motor vehicle accident this morning. They told her that it appeared to have been driver error on my part and that no charges would be laid.

She burst into tears. It was heartbreaking to watch. I wanted to comfort her, to tell her that I was all right—that I was standing right in front of her. But I was unable. All I could do was watch as she wept for some time and the officers left. She phoned our daughter, who lived nearby. Naomi immediately came over. Then my wife phoned our other children. Most were close enough that they arrived within the hour.

They grieved over my death. I guess I never realized how much they genuinely loved me. I wished I could hug them all and tell them how much I loved them. I wished I had done that more often during my life.

They cried together and comforted each other and at times even laughed a bit. They told stories about me, some of which I had never heard before. They talked about what I had done for them and about my strengths and failings. And my children comforted their mom, who seemed to be taking it the hardest.

"If only I hadn't asked him to get that medication," she said. "He was already in a hurry ... maybe it wouldn't have happened."

She began to cry.

"No, Mom," my oldest son Benny said. "You said yourself the police said it was driver error. Being in a hurry had nothing to do with it. Dad wasn't speeding at the time. For whatever reason, he just didn't see the truck. It would have happened anyway."

That helped her. After weeping some more, she went to the lamp table. She kept her reading materials there. The photo of her and me that I had dislodged from the fridge was on top of the Bible. She picked it up and stared at it. Then she went to the kitchen and looked at the fridge where it would normally be. She stared in astonishment.

She went into the living room. "Who put this photo on my Bible?" she asked the kids.

They all just looked at her. Each one denied doing it. She asked our two grandchildren. They assured their grandmother that they had not touched the photo.

She turned to Naomi. "I know that photo was not on my Bible this morning when your dad left because I read my Bible after he was gone."

Naomi was silent before replying. "Dad must have put it there after he died. He wanted you to know that he's all right," she said, a tear running down her cheek.

They hugged and cried and shared the story with the rest of the kids and grandchildren. It had worked. I had wanted to somehow communicate with them that I was OK.

There was only one problem. I hadn't put it there. The only thing I had done was knock it onto the floor.

My angel looked at me and smiled.

"You did that, didn't you?" I asked.

"No," he replied, "your wife's guardian angel did it. He knew it would bring her comfort in her time of grief. You cannot see him now, but he is here watching over your wife. And so are the guardian angels of your children and grandchildren."

That was a comfort. I stayed with my family well into the evening until they began to leave. My family was a motley crew at best and dysfunctional at worst. They were rarely unified about anything, and family gatherings where everyone was there were rare. But with the news of my death, they had all showed up and gathered peacefully. Everyone put aside their differences for at least a while. It was nice to see, and it gave me peace that they now thought I was all right.

I didn't know what to do next. I felt as if I was being beckoned by someone, but I didn't know who. The feeling started to come over me that perhaps I should move on. Maybe I had seen enough. Maybe it was time to leave.

I sat in my recliner and contemplated it. Our cat came up to me. He seemed to know I was there. I marvelled at that.

I stroked his fur. "Well, Fuzzy, I don't know what to do."

He purred. That brought me solace as I thought about my next move.

CHAPTER 4

THE DECISION

> For to me, to live is Christ and to die is gain. I am torn
> between the two: I desire to depart and be with Christ,
> which is better by far.
> —Philippians 1:21, 23 (NIV)

Should I stay or should I go? My angel had told me God granted me more
time on the earth if I so desired. I wanted to stay and help my family in
any way I could. But I was now seeing that any help I could give would
be minuscule at best. I felt as if I was being invited to move on but I was
afraid, afraid that it wouldn't be what I was hoping for. I sat for a long
time thinking about it.

I heard my wife weeping in the next room. I went to her. I wanted to
comfort her, but there was nothing I could do. I watched her phone Fred
and make arrangements for Stephen to spend the night. She was holding
herself together better than I expected.

I decided to go see my other kids again. Naomi had told the news to
my two grandchildren. They were sad but were also glad that Grandpa
was now in heaven. At least that's what my daughter had told them. I only
hoped she would prove to be correct.

I watched them get ready for bed. They were moody and grumpy and
giving each other and their mother a hard time. I remembered the days
when I had children that age. It was a lot of work, but it was beautiful.
Where had the time gone? If only I could play one more game of checkers

with my grandson. Naomi finally managed to get them tucked into bed for the night and then decompressed with my son-in-law.

I left and flew to my uncle Ron's house. He had not come over to my house after my wife gave him the news. He was on the phone with my cousin.

"Yes, Johnny was always in a hurry," he said. "I tried to tell him he was doing too much and that he needed to slow down but, no, he wouldn't listen. That's what happens."

He then offered to have my cousin come into business with him. I hadn't even been dead for twelve hours and he was already moving on.

I went to my son Benny's house. He was sad. He sat on the couch drinking a beer, staring off into space.

His girlfriend entered.

"He was a great dad," Benny said to her. "He did so much for me." Tears filled his eyes.

His girlfriend put her arms around him, and they held each other.

I wanted so badly to interact with them. I looked at my angel. He shook his head. I didn't understand why that was, but I was in no position to argue. My angel seemed to possess wisdom and knowledge far beyond mine.

I left and flew on. I visited Keith again. He too looked really sad. He was smoking with his girlfriend and blaming himself for my death.

"Dad was on his way to visit me when the accident happened. I should have told him to stay home because of the snow. If he had he might still be alive," he said as he cried.

My ex-wife and his girlfriend consoled him.

"There wasn't anything you could have done," Lindsey said. "The snow had nothing to do with it. Your dad just made a mistake, that's all. It could have happened to anybody."

Pain shot through me as I watched. I had not spent as much time with him when he was growing up as I would have liked. I was always too busy with other things. There were so many more things I wanted to do with him. I wanted to go to his graduation and his wedding. I wanted to play with his children. Now all my plans were for nought.

I left and visited my other children. All I ever really wanted to do was be a good dad and grandfather, yet I never seemed to have the time.

I was always too involved with my projects, my friends, my games and of course, my work.

I looked at my angel. "I really want to be alive again in my body. I want to finish some things in my life before I die. I don't want to be dead yet. Are you sure there isn't a way?"

"I'm sorry. There isn't. Your life in the flesh is now over. You cannot go back. Now you must decide whether to stay on the earth for a while or move on to your eternal life. It's your decision."

It was a decision I didn't want to make. I was afraid, afraid of where that eternal life might be, afraid that I had not done enough or had enough faith to be worthy of heaven. Yet it seemed that staying on the earth would be of little benefit. I figured my family would probably pick up the pieces and move on without me. There was really nothing I could do except observe them, and I really didn't see the point in that. I now knew that they all had guardian angels who could help them far better than I ever could. They were sad that I was gone but were showing strength and resilience.

"Can I visit them from where I'm going?" I asked my angel.

"I cannot answer that with certainty. But sometimes it is permitted."

I thought about it. I felt I was being summoned. "All right," I finally said. "I think I'm ready to move on."

"All right," he said. "If you're sure."

I thought about it for a moment. "I'm sure."

"Follow me."

And with that we rose into the sky.

CHAPTER 5

THE JOURNEY

For we must all appear before the judgment seat of Christ,
so that each of us may receive what is due us for the things
done while in the body, whether good or bad.
　　　　　　　　　　—2 Corinthians 5:10 (NIV)

As we rose higher and higher above the earth, I felt anything but sure. More doubts engulfed me. There were too many things in my life that I had left unfinished. I just wasn't prepared for death.

Perhaps, I thought, *I can still go back.* I had heard of near-death experiences where people experienced the world beyond for a while and then returned to their bodies. Maybe I could be one of those. Maybe it wasn't too late.

As we continued, I looked back at the earth. It was stunning. A beautiful blue and green emerald—my home.

We continued, my guardian angel leading the way. Things grew darker as we entered space. I sensed other beings near us on the same journey. I even caught glimpses of them, but I never came close enough to get a good look or communicate with them. It was like we were in a tunnel yet it really wasn't a tunnel. I did not feel afraid. My angel was at my side. But I did not know where we were going or how long it would take to get there.

After what seemed a short while, I saw a bright light in the distance. It grew stronger as we progressed. Not only could I see it, I also felt it. It was as if it penetrated all the way through me. I had never experienced anything like this. The light seemed to be alive. In fact, the light seemed to be life itself.

Suddenly I saw other beings approaching me from the same direction as the light. At first, I could not make out who or what they were, but as they came into view I knew immediately who they were. They were relatives and friends I had known during my life. They had passed away before me.

The first to greet me was my mother, who had passed away only a few years before my accident. She looked so young and vibrant! She looked full of joy and happiness. I had not seen this in my mom in the many years I had lived with her. So often she had seemed down and preoccupied with the challenges she'd faced. But now she appeared full of peace and contentedness.

She embraced me. "I'm so happy to see you!" I felt the love she had for me. I had never felt it quite like this in my fleshly life.

"Mom, I love you," I said as we hugged like we had never hugged before. She looked so brilliantly lovely and so much younger than when she had died. She looked like she had when I was a young teen.

I was greeted by my grandparents and uncles and aunts and a cousin. They all seemed so happy to see me and greeted me with more love and warmth than I ever remembered while alive. I was welcomed by two friends I thought I would never see again. They all made me feel totally at ease. It was the most joyous reception I had ever received.

Then a child appeared from the group; she was gorgeous. She stood beside my mother. She came up to me, tentatively at first, and then rushed at me and embraced me.

I looked at my mother.

"She's your granddaughter," she said.

I was surprised by that. I had no grandchildren who had died. And then it came to me: Naomi had had a miscarriage a few years earlier. It had devastated her.

I picked up my granddaughter and hugged her. "Aren't you beautiful! I'm so happy to meet you!"

I felt the love emanating between us. How precious she was. As I looked more closely, I noticed the strong resemblance with my daughter. It made me feel so joyful to know she was here with the rest of my family.

The jubilation I felt was unmatched by anything I had ever experienced. But there was one person missing, one person I would have expected to be here as well. It was someone I had been very close to during my life. He had died ten years before my mother.

"Where's Dad?" I asked her.

She smiled. "He's all right. He'll be here after a while. He's somewhere else right now."

At that, my guardian angel indicated that it was time to continue. My relatives and friends went back past the light. They said they would probably see me again soon. I did not know what they meant by that, but it was reassuring to hear.

My guardian angel gently led me toward the light. It was the most beautiful feeling I had ever had, and the light was the most dazzling thing I had ever seen. There was nothing like this on the earth—not even close.

As I neared it, I realized it was more than just a light. It was a person. I could not make out any features, but I knew it was a person.

I felt immersed in love. Warmth, tenderness, and affection enveloped me. I felt cared for and cherished. It was, by far, the sweetest, most comforting feeling I had ever had.

He was magnificent. Grandeur and splendour radiated from him. I knew who I was standing in front of. I still could not make out a distinct form, but I knew who this was. I had known my entire life that I would meet him one day. And today was the day.

CHAPTER 6

THE MEETING

For we will all stand before God's judgment seat. It is written: "As surely as I live,' says the Lord, 'every knee shall bow before me; every tongue will confess to God." So then, each of us will give an account of himself to God.
—Romans 14:10-12 (NIV)

My angel and I fell to our knees.

Jesus spoke with gentleness. "Welcome, Johnny my son," he said. "Your journey on the earth is now complete. It is time for you to begin a new state of your existence. Now we will review your life—all your actions and words. You must give a reason for the things you said and did during your earthly journey. A determination will then be made as to where you will go next."

I was in complete awe. I couldn't move or speak. I was now in the presence of the most formidable and breathtaking Being I could ever imagine. He radiated greatness and majesty. I wanted to ask him what he meant by his words, but I was so overwhelmed, I remained silent.

He spoke words filled with love and without any tone of judgment. It was obvious, however, that that was exactly what was about to happen. I did not feel a sense of dread, as I would have if a judge on the earth had said such a thing to me. Yet there was no doubt that he spoke with authority. Jesus, and Jesus alone, would render the decision as to where I would spend eternity.

The feelings of love and comfort put me at ease enough that I was compelled to speak. "Lord, thank you for all you have done for me in my life. Thank you for creating me. Thank you for the wonderful blessings you bestowed upon me. You were very good to me in my life."

I paused. I composed myself and continued. "But I feel, Lord, that I am not ready for this yet. I feel there are other things I need to finish before I move on. If I may be so bold, may I ask you, you who can do all things, if I could go back into my flesh and complete the things I need to complete?"

I was on my knees with my head bowed and my hands clasped in prayer. I did not look at the Magnificence before me. *Perhaps I should not have spoken at all,* I thought. A twinge of fear ran through me.

He replied, "Your journey on the earth is complete, my son. It is time for you to leave the flesh. You may not go back. It will be better for you and for those around you that your earthly life is ended. They will continue their journeys without your presence. Ultimately, this will benefit both them and you more than if you stayed."

I did not understand how that could be possible, but I had nothing to say. I accepted the words my Creator had said. "Yes, Lord," I replied.

"Now we will review your life, and you will see the results of your deeds and words, both good and bad. You may give a reason for them, if you so desire. After that I will determine where you will go next."

I felt uneasy about this, but I had no choice. I was before my God. There would be no going back to complete my life as I had envisioned. I knew for certain that I would not get another chance to finish the things I felt I needed to do before I died. I would never be able to fix the problems I had in my relationships with others or repay debts I owed. There would be no happy retirement spent traveling with my wife and growing old together. There would be no more time spent with my kids and grandkids as I had planned. My life was over. There would be no do-overs.

So now I faced judgment. I felt trepidation about it, but I hoped it would be all right. I had been a pretty good person overall during my life, I reasoned. Sure, I had done some bad stuff, but I thought there must have been more good than bad.

My angel and I were still on our knees before the Lord. I waited, with my head bowed and my eyes closed, for what would happen next.

C H A P T E R   7

PRIDE

God opposes the proud but gives grace to the humble.
—James 4: 6 (NIV)

Jesus spoke with kindness. "You may stand, my son, and open your eyes. The review of your life is ready to begin."

I did as he said.

And then it began, in living colour and 3D better than any screen could possibly portray it. It was as if I was actually part of the scene— except I wasn't. I only watched.

I saw my mother giving birth in a hospital delivery room. She was so happy when I was born! I was her first child. I saw my dad there too. My mother looked very much like she had when I saw her just minutes earlier. She was glowing and beautiful.

Scene after scene of my development from baby to child quickly played out. It was amazing. I literally saw myself grow up in 3D. At times I had a hard time believing it was me.

I saw my triumphs and failures. I saw the love my parents had for me when I was sick or in trouble. Not only did I see it, I felt it. The emotions of those in close contact to me could be felt by me as I viewed each scene.

I saw and felt what it was like to be my parent. I really had had no conception of what it was like to raise me. Now I saw all the work, worry, money, and time my parents spent on me as I grew up. I also saw how little gratitude I had shown them for what they had done. I saw that I thought I was special and that I deserved what they did for me—and my sense of entitlement.

In my mind I had always believed I was an easy kid to bring up, and maybe in comparison to others I was; I don't know. I now saw, however, that raising me had been no easy task, and with each scene, my appreciation for my parents grew. How I wished I had expressed that appreciation when we were all alive together.

Scenes passed. Then one appeared from my teenage years; I must have been about thirteen at the time. I had low self-esteem, but I wanted to make friends. I tried to tell some jokes, but no one laughed.

As I entered the school cafeteria at lunchtime, a couple of classmates made fun of me. "Here comes Mr. Boring," one said. "He's so boring he has me snoring!"

A chorus of laughter rang through the cafeteria. It seemed everyone had heard it. I felt crushing rejection. It felt as if everyone in the cafeteria was laughing at me. I left without eating.

It had been the most embarrassing moment of my life. The sense of rejection that I felt on that day would stay with me to one degree or another for the rest of my life. All I wanted was to have friends and be popular. Instead, I felt alone and humiliated.

Later that day at recess, the same boys were on the basketball court. They again taunted me.

I exploded in anger. "We'll see who's boring when I'm done with you," I said.

I rushed at the one who had done most of the talking. I was bigger and stronger than him and let him know it. I punched him in the face, bloodying his nose and mouth, and then grabbed him in a headlock and flung him to the ground. His friend came to stop me. I gave him a shove and walked off. I had hurt him; I felt it. I had given him what he deserved.

Watching the incident again now, so many years later, still gave me a sense of satisfaction.

Then I was shown what it had done to him. When he went home, he got more punishment from his alcoholic father. His dad gave him another beating and told him he needed to toughen up and learn to defend himself. I saw and felt his embarrassment.

When I saw him at school the next day, he was sullen and quiet. That pleased me even more. I had fixed him, I reasoned. Day after day I looked at him with disdain in my eyes. I could see my conceit.

I never apologized and never had an ounce of empathy for him for the rest of our lives. Occasionally I saw him in town, and I always gave him the same look of disdain. I hated that guy, and in my opinion, I had given him what he had coming.

I determined to never forgive him. The feeling of rejection and humiliation that I felt because of him would never leave me completely. He never apologized to me, and I doubt I would have forgiven him even if he had.

Jesus spoke. "What do you say about this, my son?"

"Well, Lord," I replied. "I kind of feel I gave him what he deserved."

"Why did you never forgive him, even after many years?"

I cleared my throat. "He never apologized, so I didn't feel as if I had to."

I soon found out that that was the wrong answer.

"That is not what I desired," Jesus said. "I shed my blood so that those who killed me on the cross could be forgiven. They never apologized for nailing my hands to that cross or flogging me or beating and mocking me. But I asked my Father to forgive them because they did not know what they were doing.

"You shed that boy's blood because you were deeply hurt by what he had done. But you never gave up the hatred that you felt for him, even though he never realized how deeply he had hurt you. You refused to forgive him even though you knew what I had said in my Word: that you must forgive even those who hate you and treat you badly. You felt justified in your unforgiveness and pride and you carried it with you to this very moment. You took it upon yourself to be his judge, even though you did not know everything about him. One day he will stand before me, and he will have to account for how he treated you. And in rendering a judgment, I will consider all the other factors in his life, factors of which you are not aware. Do you understand this?"

I would have crawled under a rock if one had been available. I understood perfectly. "Yes, Lord. I understand. I never thought about it that way before."

"Good," he replied. "Continue watching."

Another scene opened. This time I was older and beginning my life at work. My boss had gone behind my back and offered my job to another employee. Then she lied to me about it. I found out about it because my colleague told me. I hated my boss after that, and I never trusted her again. I would only speak to her when I had to. I would never give her a friendly greeting or ask how she was doing.

Then a scene opened from years later. We were both much older, and by now she had retired. She was walking her dog in the park, and I saw her there.

She spoke to me cheerfully. "How are you doing?"

I did not want to acknowledge her. "Good," I said as I looked away.

I carried on my way. I disliked her immensely and was not going to forgive her. She was a lousy person, I reasoned, and wasn't worthy of it. I saw the loathing I had for her, loathing that I still carried in my soul at this moment. But as I observed her and felt her emotions, I now saw how she felt about me. There was no hatred. There was no dislike. She seemed to have genuinely positive emotions toward me. For her, the incidents of the past seemed to have been long forgotten.

I cringed. In my pride I had refused to forgive her or even be civil toward her. I saw her reaction to my insolence. I felt her emotions of guilt and sadness at the way she had treated me. She had never apologized, but I now saw that she felt bad about it. I saw that she too probably had pride that prevented her from apologizing. I saw that I could have ended it. If I had simply been friendly and polite the entire matter would have been resolved. But I did not want to forgive her, so it never was.

Jesus spoke. "You felt justified in not forgiving her, my son, because she hurt you very deeply. In your pride, you took it upon yourself to judge what was in her heart, something you could not possibly have known. Now you see that your judgment was in error. You desired that others would judge you based on what was in your heart, yet you did not extend that same standard to her. If you had humbled yourself and forgiven her, you would have learned that you had been wrong about her. That is what I desired. Do you understand?"

I didn't know what to say. He was correct. His words pierced right through me. I hung my head. "Yes, Lord, that makes perfect sense. I was wrong. I now wish I had done things differently."

My angel stood silently beside me. I felt deep remorse. I wasn't sure I wanted to see what followed next.

CHAPTER 8

SORROW

Blessed are those who mourn, for they will be comforted.
—Matthew 5:4 (NIV)

Back on the earth, my wife was just finishing up her phone conversation with her dad. "I don't think I'll ever recover from this, Daddy," she whispered.

"You probably won't ever fully recover," he said, "but with time you'll begin to feel better. I know it hurts, and I know how painful it was for me when your mother died, but with time, the pain will diminish. It's still there every day; you think about them every day, but you will learn to move on with your life. That's what they would want from us."

Julie thought about those words as she concluded the conversation and said goodbye. They were comforting words. The problem was she wasn't sure that she really believed them.

Her life had changed in an instance. One moment life was normal. Everything was as it always had been. The next moment and a knock at the door changed her world forever.

She cried until tears would come no more. Now penetrating numbness set in. She had always suffered from small bouts of depression throughout her life, but they had always gone away with the ebb and flow of time. She wasn't sure the same would happen this time.

Her husband was dead. Johnny was her best friend and partner. He was someone she could always talk to and enjoy spending time with. They had a wonderful, fulfilling life together. He played a major role in the care of their disabled son. She too had a disability and doubted she would be able to get a job. Johnny had always managed the finances and provided most of the income. How would she and Stephen survive? It was too much to think about.

She had contemplated suicide in the past. As she lay on her bed, the old thoughts started coming back. She pushed them out as she thought about her children. That would be too much for them to bear. She had to continue, to struggle and fight. She and Johnny had always talked about how they wanted to live long enough to be at their grandchildren's weddings. Now she would have to do it and represent them both. That would be many years from now. Would she be able to make it? It seemed like an insurmountable task.

The darkness seemed to surround her, placing her in an ever more tightening grip. She would have to plan a funeral, something she had never done before. She would have to find a place to bury him, as they had never decided on that. She would have to take over all the financial matters that he had handled, something she wasn't particularly good at. It was all so overwhelming. She just wanted to stay underneath her covers and never come out again.

Hunger pangs gnawed at her. She had not eaten anything since early in the morning, before the police officers arrived. She knew she should eat.

She forced herself out of bed and went to the kitchen. Her stomach felt numb, but she managed to consume a small snack.

As she sauntered into the living room, she saw that their cat was sleeping cosily on her husband's recliner. He didn't seem to have a care in the world.

"Oh Fuzzy, how can you be so relaxed?" she asked. "Don't you know what happened today? Dad died and he's never coming back. You lay there sleeping like nothing's going on. Don't you care? Can't you sense what's happened?"

The cat looked up at her. He couldn't understand what his owner was saying, but he recognized that she was distressed. What she was distressed about he had no idea. Everything was fine in his world.

"Why did it have to happen? Why now? I don't understand."

She saw her Bible with the picture of her and Johnny still lying on it. She opened it and read, "He will wipe away every tear from their eyes, and death shall be no more, neither shall there be mourning, nor crying, nor pain anymore, for the former things have passed away."

A tear rolled down her cheek. The cat rubbed up against her and purred.

"Thank you, Lord, for that," she said. "Please help me. Please. I don't think I can handle this. And please be with Johnny. I know he's with you now. Please take care of him." She prayed as she slumped down into his recliner.

She went back to bed and buried herself under the covers, the desolation of the night her only companion. She thought about how to alleviate the pain. Did she still have those pills? She felt herself on the precipice of the abyss.

She would have to try to go on. She would have to try to push through the bleakness. She would have to try to not let the darkness overcome her. But she didn't know if she had the strength to ward it off. Maybe not this time. Maybe not ever.

CHAPTER 9

PATIENCE

The end of a matter is better than its beginning, and patience is better than pride.
—Ecclesiastes 7:8 (NIV)

As I waited, another angel arrived and presented something to Jesus.

Jesus said, "Your wife has just prayed to me to take care of you. She is suffering greatly because of your death. She is sinking into a deep depression. She has asked for my help with this."

I listened with sorrow. "Please help her, Lord. I know this is going to be overwhelming for her."

I felt the compassion coming from Jesus. "I will, my son," he said. "The Holy Spirit is comforting her. This is the most difficult trial she has ever faced in her life, and the Holy Spirit will be there to help. As long as she perseveres and relies on me, she will pass through it and in the end be strengthened by it."

That gave me some comfort. "Thank you, Lord."

After a brief pause another scene opened in front of me.

My oldest son Benny was in dreadful distress. He was sitting on a couch with a hoodie pulled up over his slouched head in his arms, resting on his knees. He wore sunglasses.

I saw myself enter the room and sit on the couch beside him. He wouldn't look at me. He wouldn't even move. I told him I was there, but there was no response. It was like he was a zombie in some sort of state of suspended animation.

I felt the emotions coming from him as I watched. They were intense: Guilt. Shame. Embarrassment. Unworthiness even to live.

I remembered this event well from my life. It had happened about fifteen years prior to my death and shortly after my dad had died. Benny had assaulted his mentally disabled brother Stephen. He had completely lost control and beaten him so badly that Stephen had to be hospitalized.

He was arrested and placed in a treatment facility. It was there that I was visiting him. He had a history of becoming violently angry and assaulting other people. Each time I had tried to get him help, but it hadn't gone well. His anger had continued to flare at the slightest perceived insult.

He had even become angry at me on several different occasions, even attacking me physically. We had come to blows, but there was never any serious injury to either of us. I had never reported it to the authorities.

He had broken my glasses, bloodied my nose and left bruises on me, but each time I forgave him. I knew he was suffering from some sort of mental disorder and that what he really needed was a proper diagnosis and treatment.

So I was patient with him. Other family and friends encouraged me to have him locked up and be done with him, but I couldn't. He was my son. I was his dad. We would get through this, whatever it was, together. I was determined that I would never, ever give up on him.

This time, however, seemed different. Stephen could not defend himself. He had made some insulting remark, as he was prone to do, and Benny attacked him. He had beaten him so badly that Stephen began to have seizures. When the doctor couldn't get the seizures to stop, he had to be hospitalized. He was there for more than a week, and there was even a time when we thought he might die.

My wife had called the police. She'd had no choice. There was no way Benny could continue to live with us under these conditions. They came and arrested him. It was a horrible, nightmarish scene. I had one son lying on the floor in a pool of blood unconscious while another was being taken away in handcuffs. It was one of the lowest points of my life.

After this incident the calls from some of my family to give up on him intensified. Let the government and experts deal with him, they said. He's never going to change, they assured me. He's a psychopath, they pronounced. Don't waste your time with him, they advised.

I thought deeply about it, but through it all one thought kept ringing true. Even though what he had done was terrible, inexcusable and unforgivable, he was still my son. I was still his dad. If I didn't try to help him, who would?

As I viewed the scene of me on the couch beside Benny, I now felt each of our emotions clearly. Although I was upset at what he had done to his brother I also felt compassion for him. I saw how much pain he was in.

I put my arms around him. "We'll get through this. It will be all right. What you did was wrong, but we'll get you the help you need. I'll help you," I heard myself say.

He still refused to look at me. We sat there for a long period. There was silence.

Finally, he spoke. He did not raise his head or look at me. "I'm a psychopath," he said.

I grabbed him by his shoulders and shook him. "Look at me," I said as I looked into his face. "Look at me!" I repeated more forcefully.

He looked up. I took off his sunglasses. His eyes were dull and sad.

"You are not a psychopath. You are a good person. You have a good heart. You made a mistake. You have a problem. But you are not a psychopath," I stated emphatically. "And never, ever let anyone tell you differently."

He began to weep. And then he openly sobbed.

I put my arms around him and held him. "I will never, ever give up on you, no matter how bad things get. I will always be there for you."

Jesus then showed me another scene that had occurred between my same two sons several years later. Stephen had called Benny a name and threatened to punch him. This time Benny reacted differently. He did not get angry or blow up.

He told his younger brother he needed to calm down or he would get into trouble. He did not strike him or even threaten to. I saw myself in the scene observing the interaction, and I felt how happy it made me. My son had changed. Through endurance and perseverance he had gotten the help he needed and slowly was learning to control his angry outbursts. He had told me that if I had not visited him in the treatment facility when I did and said what I said, he had planned to kill himself. He had told me the details of how he had intended to carry it out.

As I watched, I felt Jesus's approval. "You showed great patience and perseverance in dealing with your son and mine. At that point in his life, the evil one wanted to take him, but you consoled and comforted him. Your actions helped spare him from his grasp. This was a pivotal moment in his life. If you had not been patient with him, he might never have been able to escape the cycle of anger and bitterness he was entrapped in."

I was soothed by his words. Few people, other than Julie, agreed with what I had done.

He continued. "Because you were patient with him when he had done a very bad thing, he in turn learned to be patient with his brother when he was wronged. Just as I am patient with my children when they sin, you were patient with your son. This was very pleasing to me."

My angel put his hand on my shoulder. It felt good.

Jesus went on. "You were merciful to him when he had shown that he did not deserve mercy. In doing this you honoured me. For I am very merciful to those who have not earned mercy. Well done, my son."

That made me feel a lot better. To know I had done good in my life and that Jesus was happy about it caused me to feel a wave of peace.

But I had mixed feelings. I was also thinking about Benny at that moment. I knew my death would hit him very hard and that he wasn't really a believer. "Lord, please show your great mercy to my son. I know he often chooses the wrong path."

Jesus delayed for a moment before answering. "I will. At this very moment great mercy is being shown to him."

He didn't say anything further, but it allayed my fears. "Thank you, Lord," I said. "Thank you so much.

CHAPTER 10

DOUBT

The fool says in his heart, "There is no God."
—Psalm 14:1 (NIV)

Back on the earth, Benny opened another can of beer. It had been a shocking, awful day. The last thing he expected when he woke up this morning was that his dad would die today.

His dad had helped him so much in his life. He had always believed in him when others doubted. He had always been there for him when things looked bleak. He was always there when he needed advice, or a ride somewhere or a little bit of money.

And now he was gone. Just like that he was gone. Dad was gone, and he was pretty sure he would never, ever see him again. At least that was what he had come to believe. He didn't believe in God or a life after this one.

His dad, on the other hand, believed in God. He had told him that on many occasions. He had been very clear about where he stood on that subject—that was for sure. For Benny, however, it was different. For him there was this life and this life only.

His mom and his dad were believers. They went to church regularly and prayed before meals. They talked about God and Jesus as if they really believed they existed. It wasn't that what they said didn't make any sense to him. In fact, a lot of what they said made a lot of sense. It was just that, if he was honest with himself, he really didn't want to believe in God. After all, if he really believed in God, he would have to give up nearly all the things he liked. He liked having sex with whoever he wanted whenever he wanted with no strings attached. He liked doing drugs and getting stoned. He liked drinking booze until he was hammered. He liked being lippy with people who annoyed him and fighting with them if they became too belligerent.

If he professed belief in God, he reasoned, he would have to give all those things up. That wasn't for him. It was better to believe that God didn't exist and that he would never have to answer to anyone higher than himself.

As he sat and drank, he thought about his dad. He knew he could probably not have had a better one for him. Even though he lived a lifestyle that was the exact opposite of his dad's, his dad had always tolerated him and helped him out. He hadn't preached to him, although his father left no doubt as to where he stood on things. He hadn't been perfect, to be sure, but what person was?

The beer made him feel better. It penetrated his body and eased his pain, especially the mental pain of the loss he was feeling. He planned to keep drinking tonight until he was totally numb—totally oblivious to the sadness and heartache. It had been a horrible day, a terrible day, the worst day of his life.

As he reached for another can, a thought came into his mind. What if his dad was right about God? *What if he's in heaven right now, and that when I die someday, I can see him again?* What if he was still alive but just in a different place?

His mom and sister told the story about the photo of them on the Bible and how they thought Dad had put it there. Had he? More likely, he figured, that one of the other kids had done it and then lied about it to make everyone feel better.

He thought about these things as he became more relaxed with the effects of the alcohol. If Dad was still alive in heaven, then maybe there was more to life than having sex, doing drugs and drinking. It wouldn't make sense to say God doesn't exist if he believed his dad was in heaven. Or maybe he wasn't. Maybe everything was just one big meaningless mess.

Eventually the alcohol overwhelmed his senses and he fell into a deep sleep.

He dreamed about his dad playing pitch and catch with him as he had often done when he was younger. They were both laughing and having an enjoyable time. There was a bond between them he could almost feel. Then, suddenly, a large creature appeared. It was ugly, grey, and reptilian in appearance. It grabbed the ball and swallowed it. His dad ran from the creature. The beast beckoned for him to come and ride on him. There was a saddle on him. Then a beautiful woman holding a can of beer appeared and got onto the creature and waved for him to join her. She was very beautiful, but her face was stone cold.

In the background he heard his dad's voice yelling, "No, Benny, no! Do not go with her! Run from them Benny, run!"

He woke up in a cold sweat. The dream had been so vivid that he felt it was real.

As he calmed down, he realized it had just been a dream. That's all it was—nothing to get upset about.

He rolled over and grabbed for another can of beer. All the cans were empty. He lay awake and thought about the day and the dream.

"Meaningless," he thought, "it's all just meaningless. A big, fat meaningless mess."

There was only one certainty. He was really going to miss his dad: he would really, really miss him.

CHAPTER 11

ENVY

Resentment kills a fool, and envy slays the simple.
—Job 5:2 (NIV)

I was still thinking about Benny as I waited for the life review to continue.

Jesus knew what I was thinking. He said, "Your son and mine must choose which path he will take in his life. The Holy Spirit has sent him a dream to remind him of this. All humans must decide whether they will follow the path of good that leads to life or the path of evil, which leads to death. It is the most important decision they will ever make. All have free will. Benny still has not completely decided which path he will take. He has been shown mercy this night, and I will patiently wait for his decision. He must choose his ultimate life path before he comes before me. After that it will be too late."

I thought about that. I hoped he would change and choose a different path. I hoped I had chosen the right path. "Yes, Lord."

At that moment the next scene opened before me.

I saw myself at work. I was looking at the new hire. She was beautiful—everything I imagined in a woman. I lusted after her—that was easy enough to see. But now I felt the passion coming from me.

I got to know her as time went by. She was married. I was single. Her husband worked away from home. I had met him a few times. To me it looked like he didn't love her or look after her or their children. He was always away leaving her to take on all of the responsibilities and pay all of the bills. What he spent his money on I did not know, but I had heard he was into gambling. I was convinced he was not worthy of her. I was also convinced that I was. I thought of him and what he had, and I decided I deserved that, not him.

She was a sweet, lovely woman, and I desired her. But to have an affair was out of the question. She was too nice, too sweet. As well, an affair would violate the values instilled in me from my youth. I wasn't even willing to suggest it. I would have to wait for her to leave him, which I was convinced would happen in time.

So I bided my time. I had other relationships, but none led to marriage. At that time in my life, whenever I thought of the perfect woman, I thought of her. So I waited patiently for things to develop.

Then one day I pushed the envelope. The scene opened. I was alone with her in a parking lot. We had arranged to meet so that I could pick up a package I was purchasing from her. It was the first time I had ever been alone with her away from work.

"How are you?" I asked.

Her eyes were dazzling, her smile even more so. "I'm fine. How are you?"

"Doing well." I paused to look into her eyes.

"Well, here is your package." She handed it to me.

I handed her the money, caressing her hand as I did.

I saw myself move closer, desire welling up inside of me. I wanted to kiss her. She could sense it.

I put my hand on her upper arm. "Thank you," I said.

I could see how hard this was for her. She wanted to kiss me but couldn't bring herself to do it. She pulled away. "I have to go."

I stood there and watched her drive away. I winced as I saw the episode now so many years later. I saw the pressure I put on her because I felt I deserved her.

After that, I was possessed with thoughts of her. At work, I was always aware of where she was or what she was doing. It affected my job. Often I spent more time thinking about her than I did about my duties.

The next scene opened. It was her birthday, and I was working with her. I bought a special lunch of Italian food for her because I knew she liked it.

She ate with me, but I sensed something was wrong. And now as I watched, I saw and felt it. I saw that she was trying to repair her relationship with her husband. I also felt that she desired to be with me and that I was placing her in a quandary. I could now see the stress I was putting her under. In my lust and envy, I caused emotional pain to the woman I most desired. I was forcing her to make a choice that she would have never been forced to make if it weren't for my advances. I now saw that I was wrong. I recoiled when I saw my actions.

She pulled away from me after that and acted rather coolly around me. I got into another relationship and eventually married. Slowly I put her out of my mind. I came to feel that she really wasn't the one for me after all.

But until now, I had never felt remorse for my actions toward her and had never apologized. The feeling that I had done nothing wrong had stayed with me the rest of my life. After all, I reasoned, I had not actually committed adultery. I now saw the damage my passions had caused. It wasn't until I observed them from this vantage point and saw her emotions as well as my own that I fully realized what I had done. Until now I had not understood how much I had affected her life.

Jesus said, "You did not commit literal adultery with her, but you committed adultery with her in your heart. You knew about my admonition against this because you had read it in my Word. You never felt remorse for that. Your actions affected her attempts to reconcile with her husband and her relationships with her children and family."

I lowered my head with regret. In my pride I had always considered myself a good person. But I now realized that at times I had not been.

"I see now, Lord. My actions were wrong. I disobeyed your Word. You are correct. I knew what you had said about committing adultery in our heart, but I ignored that and rationalized that if I didn't do it literally, I hadn't done anything wrong. I now see how wrong I was. I am truly sorry."

There was nothing else to say. The evidence in front of me spoke for itself.

Jesus continued. "Out of envy you desired someone who was not yours to have. You attempted to take what was not yours instead of relying on me. This has caused a blemish on your soul, and it caused problems in the lives of others. Envy and lust always do."

I thought about what he was saying. It struck deep within me, penetrating all the way to my heart. It was the pure, unadulterated truth.

And although it was painful to hear, I welcomed it. "You are right, Lord. I never understood it like that until now. I now see what my envy and lust caused."

"You have spoken well," Jesus said. "And I now see that you understand the results of your actions and words."

What he said made perfect sense. I had never deeply contemplated it like this before. My image of myself as a good person had taken a hit. Doubt about my worthiness for heaven entered my mind. Was I ready? Was I worthy? I did not know.

CHAPTER 12

GOODNESS

Therefore, as we have opportunity, let us do good to all
people, especially to those who belong to the family of
believers.

—Galatians 6:10 (NIV)

Maybe I was worthy of heaven, but maybe I wasn't.

Another scene opened. The young man appeared to be doing well. He
was studying, and it looked as if he was in university or college. He was
dressed well and looked healthy.

As I watched, I didn't understand why or how this was part of my life
review. He was reading a book in a language I did not understand, and it
looked as if he was in a country I had never travelled to.

I was perplexed. Was this a mistake? A technical glitch? Maybe this
was supposed to be in someone else's life review.

Jesus knew my thoughts. "It is no mistake. Keep watching."

It felt as if he was amused by my thoughts. His sense of humour
lightened my mood.

The scene shifted. This time I was in my late twenties. I was reading
a pamphlet about poor children in other parts of the world. I had always
lived in a wealthy country and at that point in my life had done very little
traveling. I really knew next to nothing about the extreme poverty that
many of my fellow human beings lived in, especially children. But as I
read the pamphlet, it did something to me. For a small amount of money

every month, it said, I could provide food, clothing and an education for a poor child somewhere in the world.

At that point I was not yet married, and I was doing quite nicely on my income. I was able to save money every month and had even saved enough for a down payment on a house. I had a decent car already paid for.

I bit. *I'll do it,* I thought. I phoned the number on the pamphlet and committed myself to supporting a child. It would only cost me a few hours' wages. It felt good.

As the years passed, I always honoured that commitment. In fact, as my wages went up, I sponsored several other children as well. I had no fanciful ideas that I would ever meet these children. I did it because I felt I had been blessed and that I should share what I had with those less fortunate.

Jesus showed me the children I had sponsored over the years, many of whom were now adults. They all appeared to be doing well, albeit with the same difficulties everyone else faces in life. They appeared to be in good health for the most part; a few were even married and had children of their own. It was a joy to see them. I had seen photos of them as children, but I did not recognize them as adults.

I'd really had no idea. As the years passed, I had almost completely forgotten about the small monthly deduction on my credit card. It seemed like such a small thing. I really didn't feel like I was doing anything all that special.

Then Jesus showed me another scene. Again, I did not recognize the person. It was a woman. She must have been around twenty, but her scraggly hair and rough appearance made her appear much older. She was on the street begging. She was emaciated and wore dirty clothing. Rags would have been a better description. Flies buzzed around her while she sat. People passed by her, but she was largely ignored.

Again, I did not know why Jesus was showing me this. I didn't think I had ever seen this woman before.

He said, "This woman will soon die and be with me. She has suffered much in her short life. She did not receive the support that was given to the other children that you sponsored. She was on the list to receive help when she was a child, but there were not enough sponsors. For every one of the children who received help, many, many more never did. Many lived lives of extreme poverty and died at a young age. If you had not provided the support you did, many of the children you sponsored would have had the same fate."

I thought about this as I observed her. She was suffering terribly—far more than I had ever suffered during my life. I hadn't realized that what seemed like such a small thing to me could have such a large impact on another.

Again, Jesus spoke. "Although it seemed like a small thing to you, your sponsorships produced significant improvements in the lives of others. The small goodness's you did to them in turn enabled them to do good and benefit others. For goodness has a ripple effect. It flows like a wave in a pool from one person to the next."

That made sense.

He continued. "You lived in the wealthy part of the world during your life. Just a small amount of your money produced much good in the poorer parts of the world. You gave money out of your excess. That was good. But it would have been better if you had made sacrifices to help others as well."

Now I wished I had done more. Perhaps others could have been helped like the woman I was shown who was dying on the street. It wouldn't have taken much. I had spent plenty of money on things I really didn't need.

"I see, Lord. I could have done more. I wanted to help. I didn't understand how much my small donation was doing. I could have helped more."

I had mixed feelings. I felt good that I had aided several poor children in their lives. At least I had done that. But I now saw that what I was doing was only an afterthought. If I had really focused on what I was doing, I could have benefitted so many others.

Was I a good person or a bad one? Maybe I was a mixture of both.

CHAPTER 13

GLUTTONY

Their destiny is destruction, their god is their stomach,
and their glory is their shame. Their mind is on earthly
things.

—Philippians 3:19 (NIV)

I saw the next scene open.

"Hi, Mom," I said as I entered her house.

She was sitting at the kitchen table smoking a cigarette.

"There's shepherd's pie in the fridge." She knew how much I enjoyed
her shepherd's pie.

I headed straight there and surveyed the contents of the refrigerator.
I pulled out the pie and put a heaping helping on my plate and popped it
into the microwave. I loved eating. For me, eating was not a social activity
or a bodily necessity. It was a time of sensual pleasure to be spent alone
with myself and my food.

After I finished off one plateful, I went for another. It was delicious.

As a single man and even after I was married, I went to my mother's
house almost every day to see how she was doing. Invariably I would also
check out the fridge to see what was in there and help myself to any tasty
food that I spotted. I never asked permission. I never paid her any money
for food. After my dad died, she was living on a fixed income, but she never
complained. The thought that all that food I was consuming might be
leaving my widowed parent short of money never once entered my mind.

And I could sure eat. I was a big man during my earthly life, and if there were pleasures I enjoyed more than eating good food, they were few.

I was next shown a scene of my mom. She was sitting at the table trying to pay her bills. The problem was that there wasn't enough money in her bank account to do it. To ask her kids for money would have been unthinkable. She would never do that.

Shame burned within me as I watched. How had I been so blind for all those years? How had I been so self-centred that I had not seen what my elderly mother was going through? The same woman who had greeted me with so much love and joy when I had entered the eternal realms just a short while ago had never said a thing. She had never complained even once that I could remember. And although I was at her house almost every day for years, I never figured it out. I was too consumed with the desires of my stomach.

I ate and ate and ate. How much food I had consumed over the years I shuddered to think about. And when I wasn't eating at her house, I made sure the cupboards were always full at mine. My philosophy was to never be short of sweet and savoury snacks.

And I never was. I had a large frame, so I could pack on the pounds without it being noticeable. I was always active and hardworking, so I always told myself that I deserved to eat as much as I wanted whenever I wanted.

I spent money on food, not because I needed it for sustenance but because I simply enjoyed eating it. It was a pleasure that brought me immense carnal gratification. If things had gone badly or I was in a disagreeable mood, food was the one friend I could always count on.

But I never gave a penny to my mother for food. It was a giant blind spot that had travelled with me my entire life right up to this very moment. Now I could see how my rapacious appetite had affected her. That was bad.

It was about to get worse.

Jesus again showed me the woman in the street who was wearing rags and about to die of starvation.

"If you had spent less money on food for yourself, food that you did not need, and given it to help others, then some people such as this woman would not die. As a child, this woman would have been next on the list to be sponsored by you if you had offered it. But you were focused on your own desires. Others suffered as a result, including your own mother. Do you see this, my son?"

I was dumbfounded. I had never made the connection that my appetite for food could lead to actual harm for others. It seemed like such a small thing, so innocent. But now as I viewed it from Jesus's perspective, I saw that I had been doing actual harm.

"Yes, Lord, I see now. It never occurred to me before."

"Your motive was not to harm others," Jesus said. "To you it was a minor thing. But seemingly small actions or lack thereof can have sizable consequences. If in your heart you had considered more how to help the poor, you would have done better in following my will. Your focus was too much on your own desires and wants. I did not require that you give up everything, I only desired that your heart be more focused on helping those who had so much less than you. You did not see this during your life, but you see it now."

It was ever so clear. I did not know what to say. Others had suffered because of my feeding of my cravings, even my own dear mother. "I didn't know," I said. "You're right. It was not my intent to cause others to suffer."

One fact remained though. It was inescapable. They had suffered nevertheless.

CHAPTER 14

REFLECTION

> Now we see but a poor reflection as in a mirror; then we shall see face to face. Now I know in part; then I shall know fully, even as I am fully known.
> —1 Corinthians 13:12 (NIV)

Back on the earth, it was late on the day of my death.

After getting my grandsons settled for the night, my daughter Naomi went outside for a smoke with my son-in-law.

"They seem to be taking it pretty well," she said. "They just think Grandpa went on a trip to see Jesus. I don't think they realize yet that he's never coming back."

She lit up and took a couple of drags. "I've had a lot of bad days in my life, but this is the worst."

"It must be rough to lose a parent," her husband replied.

"It's too soon. I thought he might live to be 80 or 90 or 100 or something. I never thought he would die in his fifties. He seemed to be in pretty good health. Never smoked. Didn't drink. A little fat, but not too bad," she said.

"Now not only have I lost a parent, but the boys have lost a grandpa."

They were both silent for a few moments. Cigarette smoke filled the air.

"I don't know if Mom will be able to handle Stephen by herself. We'll have to help her. We'll have to go over there more. I've just been so busy lately I haven't had time."

"Ya," her husband said, "you're right."

"We'll have to be the ones to help her. Nobody else is going to be able to do it. Benny isn't capable of it and Keith is too young."

She paused for a moment and continued. "I just talked to him a few minutes before he died. I was probably the last person he ever talked to."

They finished their smokes and went to bed. She couldn't sleep. She just kept thinking about her dad and the last conversation they'd had. He seemed fine—his usual self. Always busy and always going somewhere. She believed he was all right. He must have put that photo of him and Mom on her Bible to let them know. He was probably in heaven right now singing with the angels.

Naomi believed that, although she had never acted on her beliefs. She never openly talked about them, and she certainly never went to church. That wasn't for her. Besides, her husband had had a bad experience in church when he was younger, and he had vowed never to go back. She would have to go by herself, and that wouldn't work out. Besides, all those people at church were so judgmental. *I wouldn't have any friends there,* she thought, *and nobody would like me.* She had been forced to go when she was young, but as soon as she was of age to make her own decisions, she had stopped. And she had never gone back.

She wept.

It was a sleepless night of tossing and turning, a night of sorrow and crying, a night of reflection on the deep things of life and questions about why things had to be the way they were.

"Be with my dad," she whispered to God.

She hadn't prayed since she was a child.

"Please be with him and let us see him again someday."

A peace came to her after she uttered those words. They helped mitigate the pain. Sleep finally came after that, and for a few hours at least the horrible events of the day were forgotten.

CHAPTER 15

WRATH

Do not be quickly provoked in your spirit, for anger
resides in the lap of fools.

—Ecclesiastes 7:9 (NIV)

Another prayer arrived for Jesus.

"Your daughter Naomi has prayed for you," he said.

That surprised me. Naomi had not really seemed interested in the
spiritual things of life.

"Please be with her, Lord," I said.

"I will, my son. She wants to help your wife look after Stephen. This
pleases me, and I will help her with that."

He paused for a moment. "Stephen can be difficult at times. Now I
will show you some moments from your interactions with him that will
partially explain why."

I didn't know what to expect. I had generally gotten along well with
Stephen, or so I thought. I had to admit, though, that we'd had our
moments.

"Yes, Lord," I said.

And then it continued.

I was shown Stephen, now in his early teens, glaring at me with a look
of hatred that I had not often seen in him.

I had told him to do his chores and eat his breakfast.

"You can't cook good," he said to me. "You can't cook as good as
my mom."

"Well, she's not here today, so you're going to have to eat it."

He didn't like my reply. "I'm not eating that."

I stared at him. He stared back.

"If you don't eat it, I'm going to take away your guitar," I said, referring to his most prized possession in the world.

He came undone. "Do you want me to punch you?" he said, raising his fist as he approached me.

I grabbed his raised arm. Now I was mad. "You're not going to punch me. I am your dad, and you're going to treat me with respect!" I yelled at him.

He grabbed my shirt with his free hand, ripping the pocket. It was one of my favourites.

"Let go of my shirt!" I yelled. "You just ripped it!"

I tried to free his hand, but he held on to it like a hungry dog hanging on to a bone. He had the look of a madman. And then he twisted harder.

I pushed him back, knocking him down on the couch. I put my hand over his face.

"Let go of me and I'll let you up," I yelled again.

It didn't work. He became even more defiant. "Get off of me or I'm going to punch you," Stephen said.

He punched me in the stomach and caught me in the face, knocking my glasses off. I grabbed his free hand and sat on him. He spit in my face.

That was it. I was enraged. I freed myself and got up and went to his room and grabbed his guitar.

"You see this?" I shouted. "This is what you get when you act like that!"

I took that guitar and smashed it against the bricks of the fireplace again and again and again. I did it until all that remained were splinters of wood and mangled guitar strings. Then I threw it on the floor.

I glared at him.

He started to cry. And then he came at me again, only this time it wasn't with punches but with bitter vitriol. "You are a terrible dad. You are not my dad. I hate you!" he shrieked at me.

Then he turned and left.

I went to the kitchen. In my mind I had taught him a lesson. That would teach him to treat me with disrespect. I wasn't going to allow him to treat me like that. Yes, he was adopted, but I had adopted him at a young age, and I was the only dad he had ever known or ever would know.

A new scene opened. It was the next day. Stephen was depressed. He was at school, and he was telling anyone who would listen why he was depressed. His teachers were appalled. What kind of a monster would destroy the most prized possession of a disabled child?

I saw the pain and sorrow this had caused him. He was not his usual happy-go-lucky self. The teachers tried to get him to participate in things at school, but he refused. They blamed me.

Finally, I was summoned to the school for a meeting. The teachers outlined every detail of the confrontation as they had heard about it from Stephen. They looked at me with utter condescension.

I was embarrassed, but I wasn't about to apologize. "You don't know what it's like to live with that kid," I told them. And then in so many words I went on to tell them to mind their own business and I left.

As I saw the scenes that unfolded over the following days, I saw the damage I had done to my son's psyche. He slowly recovered to his previous self, but it took a long time. I also saw how proud I had been of my wrath. Although the odd pang of guilt assailed me at times, I stuck to my assertion that I had been right in my actions.

I never did make amends for smashing that guitar. I always felt justified in doing it. At least until now. As I stood before Jesus, my confidence that I had acted correctly dissipated.

He spoke. "Your anger on that day did not produce what you wanted from Stephen. You wanted him to respect you, but your rage at his disrespect for you did not teach him that. As a result, you struggled with that attitude in him your entire life."

I silently listened, thinking about the words Jesus was speaking.

"You see, fits of rage will not teach others to respect you. They may fear you, but they will not truly respect you. Being firm and patient and having self-control will eventually gain their respect. Wrath may force others to do what you want them to do for a time, but it will never garner true respect. Only with love can that be gained. Causing fear in others will only give you the illusion of respect. Love, on the other hand, would have given you the true respect that you desired from your children. Do you understand this, my son?"

His words struck at the core of my being.

"I see now, Lord. I was wrong."

I had no way to justify my actions. I loved Stephen, and I guess that love is what got us through the remaining years of my life—that and his incredible willingness to forgive me for just about anything, even the destruction of what he loved most in the world. But at this moment I now understood that our relationship could have been so much better. If only I had been willing to give up my anger and stop trying to justify it. It saddened me to think I had been this way for my entire life and that I had never really rectified it. Most times I just rationalized my anger away. It occurred to me that maybe some of the problems that were happening between my children were a result of this.

I thought about my disabled son. He was such a blessing to me and my wife. He was an adult now, but he had never lost his childhood innocence. I wondered how he would handle my absence in his life.

I looked at my angel. He just looked straight ahead and did not speak. This wasn't good, I thought, as I waited for what would come next.

CHAPTER 16

INNOCENCE

And he said: "I tell you the truth, unless you change
and become like little children, you will never enter the
kingdom of heaven."

—Matthew 18:3 (NIV)

As it turned out, Stephen was handling my absence just fine, at least for
now. He had gone over to our respite worker's house for the night. Julie
had been in no state to look after him after the events of the day.

He had cried and hugged and told stories with the rest of the family
after learning of my death. He was sad like everyone else, but for him the
circumstances were crystal clear. His dad had died and was now in heaven.
When he died, he would go there too, and then we would be together
again. In this he was confident.

He was a 22-year-old man with the mental functioning of a 5-year-old
boy. But in this situation, he had wisdom beyond his years. He had not
one shred of doubt. He was rock solid in his beliefs.

He and Fred sat in the living room.

"Your dad was very good to me," Fred said. "I'm going to miss him."

"My dad was the best ever," my son replied, "He's in heaven now. I'm
going to miss him, but I will see him again when I die."

"Yes, you will," his worker said.

"God will look after my dad. Jesus too. My grandma and grandpa are
there also. Did you know that?"

"Yes, I knew that."

"Did you know that when people go to heaven, they have angels that take them there?"

"Yes, I knew that."

"Did you know that angels have wings? You didn't know that, did you?"

"No, I knew that."

Stephen was just getting rolling. "Did you know that in heaven, people cannot die anymore or get sick or get into accidents? Did you know that?"

"Yes, that's true."

"I want to go to heaven and be with my dad and my grandma and grandpa someday," my son said. "But for now, I have to stay here and look after my mom. She's really sad."

"Yes, she is. It's hard to lose someone you love. That's very good of you to look after her."

"I love my mom. She's the best mom ever."

Stephen then asked Fred if he could watch some of his favourite shows. He did that until it was late and time for bed.

He was sad about his dad, but it was not an overwhelming sadness. He was sure that he knew where he was and that he was OK. He was convinced that it was now his job to look after his mom now that his dad was gone. That's what his dad would want him to do. And that's exactly what he would do.

CHAPTER 17

HUMILITY

Before his downfall a man's heart is proud, but humility comes before honour.

—Proverbs 18:12 (NIV)

It wasn't that I had always reacted with anger in my life. Often, I hadn't.

The next scene opened.

My uncle Ron was on the phone. He was talking to me, and he was not happy. I listened patiently to his concerns, being careful not to contradict him or say anything negative. I had by now experienced his explosive anger on several occasions.

"You aren't doing your part. What are you getting paid for?" he said to me.

I did not respond. I just let him vent. That seemed to be the best strategy.

He went on. "I don't know if this business is going to work out. I have to do everything myself. There's nobody to help me."

My uncle had approached me many years earlier to go into business with him. I had been close with him at times in my life and he trusted me. We were only a few years apart in age. I was still single and working a full-time job and had some free time to devote to it. He knew I had some money saved up and that I had a pretty good mind for numbers, neither of which he possessed. He had an idea for a business but needed a partner.

"Fifty-fifty," he had said. "Split it right down the middle."

I made it clear that I would be doing it on the side and that I wasn't going to give up my job. I said I would only be involved doing paperwork, dealing with the government and payroll. I wasn't going to be a salesman. He agreed. So I invested the five thousand dollars from my savings account to get the business started.

Years passed. Ups and downs occurred, but overall the business prospered. Ron became increasingly difficult to deal with as time went on, however. He didn't feel that I was worthy to continue receiving half of the profits as the business grew. He was often short and unpleasant with me when we talked, and he accused me of taking advantage of him. He asked on several occasions if he could get my cousin to buy me out. I was agreeable to that, but the price I proposed was always too high. He thought I was being greedy and that I should pretty much walk away with nothing.

I had worked many hours on the business, hours my uncle either didn't see or didn't care about. I worked for no pay for nearly two years when the business was going through a rough patch. Twice I infused large chunks of cash into the business from my line of credit to keep it going because I knew if I didn't, the business would not survive. I was not one to blow my own horn, but one thing I wasn't going to do was walk away with nothing. Despite my uncle's negative attitude toward me, I always believed he had the right attributes to succeed if we would only stick with it.

So I persevered. I kept my mouth shut for the most part and patiently endured his attacks and condescending remarks. I knew that if I attacked him back, that would likely lead to an end to the business. At times I wondered if it was really all worth it. I even asked him to buy me out at one point, but he refused.

Then one day things seemed to come to a head.

The scene opened. I remembered it well. I was working on the books in my makeshift office in my home. My uncle came over. He was angry, and it was obvious it was at me. He came into my office but did not sit.

He looked at me with a scowl. "You don't do enough for this business for what you're getting paid. I'm the one who does all the work."

I looked at him. "What do you think I'm doing right now?"

"Nothing!" he shouted.

With that he rushed to my desk and pushed all my paperwork onto the floor. Then he opened the drawers of my filing cabinet and started throwing the files all over the room.

I sat there and watched in disbelief. The man was out of his mind.

Then he stormed out of my house and slammed the door.

I sat there for a few minutes contemplating what I had just witnessed. I slowly began to pick up the papers and put them back into the files. After an hour or so I had the mess cleaned up. I proceeded to finish up the paperwork I was working on when he arrived.

Several days passed. I did not contact him, and he did not contact me. When he finally contacted me, it was about a routine matter with the business. I simply talked to him in a matter-of-fact manner, as if the incident had never occurred. I had maintained my poise throughout the entire episode, and I continued to do so now.

I saw no reason to confront him about his behaviour. I did not criticize or question him about it. He never apologized, and neither of us ever talked about it the remaining years of my life. It was not that I was afraid of him—not at all. I truly cared about my uncle, and I wanted what was best for him. I felt the business benefited both of us and that it was incumbent upon me to keep it going even if I had to endure his unpleasant behaviour.

The years went by right up until this day, the day of my death. We continued in business together, and although we had the occasional dispute, we seemed to get along better as time went by.

I never held a grudge against him for the way he treated me. Deep down I liked Ron, and I never took any of his insults or actions too personally. He seemed to mellow as time passed and even seemed to be interested in the spiritual at times.

Jesus spoke to me. "You humbled yourself in the face of unjust criticism and did not retaliate. By controlling your emotions, you helped your uncle learn how to better control his. Although you didn't realize it, you were slowly influencing him as the years went by. He learned by your actions. Humility is like a wave that keeps hitting the rocks over and over. Eventually it wears down the rough edges and makes them smooth. In the same way, you helped smooth out that part of your uncle's character by humbling yourself when you were attacked. Attacking him back would have had no effect—in fact, it would have made things worse. Your actions were very pleasing to me. Well done, my son."

Jesus's words were comforting. They felt good. "Thank You, Lord," I said.

I thought about my uncle. I hadn't seen him at my house when the family gathered after my death. Maybe he didn't feel comfortable there, or maybe he didn't care. I didn't know.

But I felt better; at least for now. My motives may not have always been right, but at least I had acted in the right way. There must be some good in me. I took solace in that.

CHAPTER 18

AMBIVALENCE

With the tongue we praise our Lord and Father, and with it we curse men, who have been made in God's likeness. Out of the same mouth come praise and cursing. My brothers, this should not be.

—James 3:9-10 (NIV)

Ron was thinking about his nephew Johnny. After he hung up the phone with Johnny's cousin, he had time to give thought to his relationship with his nephew over the years. It had been good and bad at various times. Some days he cursed the fact that he had ever asked Johnny to be his partner, and other days he was glad about it. In his view, his nephew had taken advantage of him, but he had also done some good. After all, Johnny had been the one to put up the money to start the business. He had also loaned money to the business a couple of times when things were tough. Overall, he hadn't been too difficult to work with.

And he had to admit that most of the time Johnny was decent to him. He did a good enough job keeping the books balanced, dealing with the lawyers and accountants and doing the payroll. He really couldn't complain about that. It was that nagging feeling that Johnny was taking more from the business than he was putting into it that got to him. He had no proof, but he felt it was true.

But now it was over.

Just like that, it was over.

He would have to see Johnny's wife tomorrow and offer his condolences.

He would also have to discuss his nephew's share in the business, for surely that must have been left to her.

A twinge of fear hit him. Julie had been rather cool to him over the years. He knew she disapproved of some of the things he had said to his nephew. She might not be the easiest person to deal with. She could make his life very difficult if she refused to sell Johnny's share of the business for a reasonable price.

Some regret began to enter his mind. He knew he had been harsh at times. He had never apologized for the things he had said and done. In retrospect, he wished he had acted differently. He had never foreseen the possibility that Johnny would die before him and that if he wanted to obtain his half of the business, he would have to deal with his wife. He had gotten to know her over the years, and his impression was that she might be a tough negotiator.

He knew that was of his own doing.

This wasn't how he had wanted their partnership to end. Over time, he had come to have a certain respect for Johnny, and he felt overall that their partnership was in both of their best interests. He wasn't ready for it to end—certainly not like this.

But as yet, he had not shed a tear since hearing about the accident. As he dozed off, he thought about what he would say to Julie when he saw her tomorrow and the implications for the business moving forward.

He would have to look out for himself, he reasoned, because no one else would. That's the way life had been for him. And he doubted it was going to change now.

CHAPTER 19

LUST

Dear friends, I urge you, as aliens and strangers in the
world, to abstain from sinful desires, which war against
your soul.

—1 Peter 2:11 (NIV)

Unfortunately, the good feelings I had about how I had handled things with
my uncle didn't last, because Jesus now focused on a different area of my life.

The scene opened.

She was a beautiful young woman. Her hair was long and black, her
face a masterpiece of feminine loveliness. Her dark eyes sparkled when she
smiled her radiant smile. Her comely body was shaped to what I considered
perfection.

But there was a sadness about her. I observed that she had been
drinking and had been taking some sort of drugs. She seemed lonely, and
I felt that she was filled with guilt. She was not happy.

I did not know why I was being shown this. I did not recognize her
from my time on the earth. But I knew this was no mistake. Somewhere
in time our lives had intersected, and I had impacted her in some way. I
had an uneasy feeling that it wasn't for the better.

Then the scene shifted. It was me in my bedroom looking at photos in
a magazine. As I looked more closely, I saw that the photos I was looking
at were of the beautiful young woman. She was nude. I was pleasuring
myself by fantasizing about being with her. I cringed.

During my younger years, I had not considered it wrong to do this.

After all, I reasoned, these were just natural desires, weren't they? What harm could come from it? But as I grew older and matured and married, I felt more and more guilt and shame for my actions. My conscience would not let me rest.

Eventually I came to the point where I was disgusted with myself. After I went through a divorce, the old habits returned. I cried out to God to deliver me from my desires. I had hit the wall. I told God that I wanted to change and never engage in that behaviour again. Two days later I met the woman I would spend the rest of my life with.

I had never thought that what I was doing was harmful to others. I thought that if any harm was being done it was only to my spirit.

Then I saw the beautiful woman again. She was accepting cash after a photo shoot from someone who looked less than reputable. She took the money, which appeared to be quite a bit, and left, but I sensed the guilt and shame that went with her. She did not want to be doing this; I could feel it. She wanted out but felt trapped.

Suddenly it hit me like a ton of bricks. By my buying that pornographic magazine, I had directly contributed to her shame and guilt. I had paid money, a portion of which would eventually be paid to her, to look at her in the nude. If no one such as myself ever bought those magazines, there would be no disreputable characters around to entice young women like her to undress and pose for money. She would never have been involved in a lifestyle that was detrimental to her mentally, physically, emotionally and spiritually.

I saw that in my lust and desire for pleasure I had caused her to suffer. She wasn't just a photo in a magazine. She was a real, living, breathing human being who deserved to be treated with dignity and respect. She had been involved in a lifestyle that she didn't want to be involved in but didn't know how to break out of. It was a lifestyle that I had kept feeding by buying those magazines. I felt like a sadist.

I was staggered. What had I done? How many countless women had I had an effect on by paying to look at their photos and videos? How much damage had I caused in their lives?

I closed my eyes and hung my head, slowly moving it back and forth. I could not bear to see any more. This was bad—really bad. What could I say to this? Surely I deserved punishment.

I was silent.

So was Jesus for what seemed like a long while.

Then he spoke. "People do things in secret that they think are harmless to others. But every sin has an influence on others even when it is done in secret. By fulfilling your lustful desires, you contributed to injury to others. The day you felt the deep remorse and shame for your sin I heard your cries for deliverance. I forgave the wrongs you had committed, even though at that time you did not fully comprehend the depth of them. That's when I rewarded you with your wife, the woman I selected for you to spend the rest of your life with. You can now see that your actions caused damage to others—much more than you had ever imagined. You now see the full consequences of your sin. Can you understand this, my son?"

It was crushing. Whenever I had felt remorse for my actions, it had always been because of what it was doing to me—my guilt, my shame and my self-image. I had not considered the harm I might be doing to others. It had never occurred to me that I might be imposing that same guilt, shame and poor self-image on them as well. But I could now see that that was precisely what I had done.

I said, "Yes, Lord, I understand now. I see how selfish and wrong my actions were, and I see I was doing real harm to those women—something I never thought of until now. I'm truly, truly sorry. I feel so ashamed."

I had been so blind. And I had conveyed that blindness with me right into the afterlife.

Jesus replied, "You have been forgiven for fulfilling your lustful desires. But lust can leave a harmful stain on your soul until you understand the depth of it and truly begin to fight it. It requires a struggle to overcome lust—a struggle you were not finished with when you died. Nearly all humans have some kind of lust they must fight against. Now you can fully grasp yours and perceive the evil it was bringing about in your life and the lives of others."

Jesus allowed me time to contemplate what he had said. Now I only hoped that my actions would not land me in hell. For now, that seemed like a real possibility. I shuddered. All was silent. I still felt warmth and tenderness coming from him, but now the thought occurred to me that maybe he felt that way about all his creatures, even those destined to perish in the flames. A wave of fear swept over me.

The silence ended. A new scene appeared in front of me.

CHAPTER 20

SLOTH

The way of the slothful man is a hedge of thorns: but the
way of the righteous is made plain.

—Proverbs 15:19 (KJV)

I was happy the last few scenes were over, but I was soon to see that my
wrongdoings with regard to the opposite sex were not.

My ex-wife was sitting alone. She was expressionless, sad and depressed,
and all by herself—again.

Then I saw myself out golfing with my buddies. I spent time with them
instead of with her. I was enjoying myself, laughing and talking and having
a great time. I came home expecting her to have cooked a good meal for
me. I didn't kiss her when I came in the door or even give her a pleasant
greeting. I saw the disdain I exhibited toward her. She was my wife, but by
that point I had given up on our marriage. I felt that she had checked out
on me long before, and I no longer felt like I had an obligation to act like
a loving spouse. The feelings I felt so long ago now came to life in front of
me in vivid detail.

At that point in our marriage I thought Lindsey had done very little
to try to be a good wife. I'd had hopes of a wonderful, lifelong marriage,
but I quickly found out that that wasn't going to happen. From day one
it seemed that she had decided she was going to do as she pleased and do
very little for me. She gained weight and made no effort to keep herself
attractive, as she had when we were dating. It was as if she wasn't interested
in sex, and she often dressed in the same drab clothes day after day, even

sleeping in them at times. Eventually it got the point that she rarely cooked, leaving me to cook my own meals. And she had no problem pointing out my flaws.

I didn't love her anymore and felt justified in my feelings and actions.

As I watched the scenes unfold, it was obvious that I had decided to no longer do anything to try to fix the marriage. I sat on the couch and watched TV, eating the food I had prepared for myself. We had become roommates—except roommates generally like each other.

I remembered the next scene clearly. I confronted her on the deck one day.

"What is it that will make you happy?" I asked.

"A divorce," was her quick reply.

That's all she said as she went into the house and slammed the door.

Our relationship deteriorated further from there. Within the year I had granted her request, and we began the long, painful process of divorce. I saw that I was pleased about it. As far as I was concerned, she hadn't treated me very well, and the situation was of her own making. It wasn't on me.

Then another scene opened.

I was shown a little girl. She was blonde and cute. I didn't recognize her at first, but I did recognize her parents. They were much younger looking than when I knew them. They were my future in-laws, and the little girl was Lindsey.

"Get to work, you little witch!" her mother screamed at her.

Lindsey ran to a room in another part of the house as her dad came in the door.

"You'd better go find that little brat," her mom shouted at him, "or you'll be fixing your own supper."

My future wife was just a child, but she was being expected to cook supper for her dad. She had told me the stories about how her mother had talked to her and basically treated her like a slave when she was young. Now I saw, right in front of me, the brutal treatment she had received.

Day after day I saw scenes of her mother verbally and physically abusing her, her siblings and her father. She rarely relented. The little girl I would eventually marry had had a terrible childhood and a very poor role model of what a mother and wife should be. Of course, she had told me some of these things during our relationship, but until I now saw them so graphically portrayed in front of me, I did not understand the profound hurt and trauma she had experienced.

As I watched, it all came to fruition in my mind. It all began to make sense. Lindsey acted as she did in our marriage because she was copying her role model—her own mother. But in her mind, I could see that she thought she was treating me well. After all, wasn't she treating me far better than her mom had treated her dad? She didn't physically abuse me at all, and the verbal shots she gave me were far fewer than what her mother had launched at her father. She was a far better wife than her mother had been. At least that's the way she saw things.

The problem was, I hadn't seen things that way. To me she was just being lazy, so I eventually decided to be lazy in return. I reasoned that she would just have to learn her lessons the hard way. I wasn't going to try any harder to fix this mess. To me she was just being hard headed, stubborn and obstinate, and any efforts I had made to help our relationship seemed to go nowhere. I felt I had done my best to honour my marriage vows, but it seemed as if she wasn't interested. So I gave up. I decided to play the same game she was playing.

Another scene opened from many years later. By this time we had been divorced for a long time and were both in our fifties. She was sitting in her recliner, and she was alone. She looked sad and despondent, just as she had so many years ago. Tears fell from her eyes.

"Why, why did my life turn out this way?" she cried to herself. "I tried my best, and he still abandoned me. He never really loved me."

She put her hands to her face and wept. In her view life had not been fair to her. Her husband had left and married someone else. He had destroyed her life. That person was me. I felt her thoughts and emotions through her tears.

I felt remorse as I viewed the scene. I now saw that perhaps I could have done more to try to solve our marital problems. Maybe all she needed to be a good wife was a little more patience and tenderness. Maybe I had thrown the towel in too soon. Maybe I had just been too lazy and proud to do it.

Jesus spoke. "You made a judgment about her, my son, but you did not have all the facts. Thus, your judgment about her was incorrect. Laziness was not the reason she treated you as she did. The trauma she suffered as a child was the major factor. Your decision to be slothful, because that's what you perceived she was doing to you, was not what I desired. My desire was that you would have continued to make sacrifices for her even though it was causing you to suffer. This would have helped her to see me in you, and it would have strengthened her faith, which was wavering."

What He said was astonishing. Lindsey had stopped going to church and given up her Christian faith after we divorced. It was appalling to think that my actions might have played some part in that.

Again, Jesus let me contemplate in silence. As I stood there, I knew there weren't going to be any do-overs. The soul I was now was the exact same soul that had lived in my fleshly body. I was who I was. It wasn't going to change now. I could see that.

I thought about Lindsey and what being married to me must have been like for her. I now had a different perspective.

"Lord, I pray for her. I pray that my actions don't affect her eternal destiny."

Jesus responded. "They won't. She will be held accountable for her own actions and choices, not yours. You will be held accountable for your actions. All people are responsible for the choices they make in their lives. Her eternal destiny will be determined by the choices she makes, even if those choices are influenced by others."

"Yes, Lord," I said. I don't know that made me feel any better. I knew my eternal fate would soon be decided. A feeling of emptiness overcame me.

CHAPTER 21

DESPAIR

Judge not, that you be not judged. For with what judgment
you judge, you will be judged; and with the measure you
use, it will be measured back to you.
—Matthew 7:1–2 (NKJV)

I held my head in my hands in discouragement. Surely, I would not go to heaven. Surely I was lost. I had lived my life like I was on a rocket ship. I was always in a hurry to get to the next thing. Too often I had put my own selfish interests first at the expense of others. Too often I was in such a hurry to do what I thought was the right thing that I had not considered the feelings of others and had trampled on them.

My angel approached me. He said, "The review is not over. Do not despair. I was with you your entire life and saw every action you did and heard every word you spoke. You did and said much good."

I was unable to look at him. "Well, I hope you enjoyed it," I replied. "I never realized what I was doing, and now it's too late."

The angel paused for a moment. "It is too late to go back and live your life over, that is true. Now you are seeing the true consequences of your actions and words. You are seeing how what you said and did affected others. As you have been shown it was not always good. But we have only seen part of your life. You need to watch the rest."

I looked at him. "I don't want to. This is too hard. Why does it have to be so hard?"

My angel looked at me with kindness. "Every life review and judgment is unique. You are being judged based on how you judged others. At times your judgment of others was harsh. That is why you feel it is hard now for you. But I also know that at other times you were easy on others. That is why you must watch the rest."

I remained slouched over. Thoughts swirled around my mind. I had always thought of myself as being a good person, always thinking that if heaven really existed, I would certainly go there when I died. It never occurred to me that I might not be worthy or that I might be bad enough to be thrown into the flames.

At least not until now.

I knew the life review was accurate. I could not deny anything I had seen. Many of my actions had been harmful to others. At times I had been a bad person—plain and simple. And now it was too late to change it.

"I don't know if I want to see the rest," I said to my angel. "Maybe you should just take me to wherever I'm going and be done with it."

He didn't reply.

Then Jesus spoke. "Stand up, my son."

I slowly raised my head and stood on my feet. I felt His grandeur and love. I still felt compassion coming from him.

"Your life review is not over," He said. "You must now see the remainder."

I paused for a moment. "It doesn't seem like there's any point. It's obvious I treated others badly. I made a mess of things."

Again, Jesus was silent for a moment as my words hung in the air. "Many people have made messes of their lives, my son, and they are in heaven right now. It is true that you made many mistakes, but you also did many things well. Now it is time for you to see the rest of your life review. Remain standing and watch."

I did as He said. There was nothing else I could do. My angel stood beside me. The words that had been spoken to me had been a comfort. At least I had that.

CHAPTER 22

COURAGE

Have I not commanded you? Be strong and courageous.
Do not be terrified; do not be discouraged, for the Lord
your God will be with you wherever you go.
—Joshua 1:9 (NIV)

We watched the next scene open.

I saw myself at work. I was in a staff meeting. The owner of the business was addressing us. He was a stern and ruthless man who had a reputation for bullying people until he got what he wanted.

"The store will be opening on Sundays in a couple of weeks," he stated. "Everyone will be expected to work some Sundays. No exceptions."

This came as quite a shock. We lived in a small rural community where all of the businesses traditionally stayed closed on Sundays. I saw my co-workers' emotions. Most didn't like the idea. I saw and felt their reticence. I also felt their fear of this man. They seemed ready to reluctantly comply.

By this time in my life I had remarried and had older children. My wife tended to be more religious than me. We attended church every Sunday. It was also our day for spending time with family. I knew this was going to cause me a dilemma.

When I told Julie about it, she was not happy. "That's just wrong," she said. "Sunday is supposed to be a day of rest—a sacred day. All he's thinking about is money."

"Ya, you're right," I replied, but without much enthusiasm.

I wasn't as strong in my faith as Julie was, but I thought she was right.

The problem was that I feared what my boss might say or do if I refused to work on Sundays. I had a good job in a management position, and I didn't want to lose it. It had been difficult to obtain, and it paid well. I needed the money to support my wife and children.

I struggled with my predicament for days. Finally, it came to a head. The schedule was out for the following week, and I was on it to work Sunday. I didn't want to do it. But I also didn't want to tell my boss that I wouldn't.

I lay awake most of the next night thinking about what I should do. In my distress I started reading the Bible, something I hadn't been doing a whole lot of. I opened it up. Almost immediately I came across the story of Shadrach, Meshach and Abednego in the book of Daniel. It was about three men who were commanded by the king to bow down to an image of him and to worship. They said they would not. They said they only bowed down to God and him alone. The king was enraged. He told them he would have them thrown alive into a fiery furnace if they would not comply. They still refused.

"We do not need to defend ourselves before you in this matter," one told him. "If we are thrown into the blazing furnace, the God we serve is well able to save us from it, and he will rescue us from your hand, O king. But even if he doesn't, we want you to know, O king, that we will not bow down or worship the image you have set up."

The king was so infuriated by their answer that he had the furnace heated seven times hotter than normal and then had them thrown alive into the flames. But God rescued them. Not a hair on their head was singed.

As I thought about the story, I saw the parallels with what I was facing. I wouldn't get thrown alive into a furnace, but I might lose my job and income. I wasn't confident I could easily get another job—especially one that paid as well and had the benefits I enjoyed. As I thought about it, however, I realized it was more important to obey God than men. I would tell my boss the next day that I wouldn't be working on Sundays.

When I saw him in the office the next morning, he wasn't in a good mood. Sales were down, and as far as he was concerned, that was the fault of management, like me. In his mind, opening on Sundays would improve sales.

As I viewed the scene, it seemed like it had just happened yesterday.

"What would you like?" he asked, not looking up from the paper he was reading.

"I saw on the schedule that I'm supposed to work on Sunday. I've talked to my wife, and we've decided I shouldn't. We consider Sundays to be sacred. So I won't be coming in on Sundays."

He looked up at me. I saw and felt the anger coming from him.

"I don't care what you or your wife think. Either you work on Sundays or find another job."

I looked at him for a moment. "OK, then. I guess I'll be looking for another job," I said firmly.

He wasn't impressed.

I saw that his first thought was to fire me on the spot. I felt him contemplating it. But I also felt something else coming from him that I had never been aware of before: respect. He begrudgingly had respect for the stand I was taking.

"All right then, fine," he finally said. "You don't have to work on Sundays. But you'd better make sure sales don't drop off in your department. And you'd better put in more hours on the other days of the week. Now get out of my office before I change my mind."

I felt relief. I knew I could work extra hours if I had to, and I felt confident that sales in my department would not drop off. I had done it. I had stood my ground, and my boss had backed off. At least that's what I thought. But I was soon to learn that my troubles were only beginning.

Things went well at first. There were few problems, and things ran smoothly in my department.

But my boss saw things differently. He appointed one of my colleagues to look after my department on Sundays. He said it wasn't being looked after properly.

Then came the gut punch. The scene opened in front of me. I was working with my colleague when he informed me that he was being trained to take over my job. I saw his pride over this. I felt his antipathy toward me swirling around like hot flames. I had been thrown into the fire just like the three men in the story in Daniel.

I went home that night deeply depressed. I was going to lose my job. I knew it.

I prayed that night to God. My prayer life had been spotty at best. I told him that I did not want to lose my job, but if I did, I did. I told him I was not going to start working on Sundays now no matter what happened.

The next day when I went back to work, I was at peace. Weeks passed and nothing happened. My colleague continued to act toward me in a prideful fashion. My boss was cold and indifferent. But I wasn't fired. It seemed as though things were in a state of suspended animation.

Then another sudden turn occurred. My colleague who was being trained to replace me unexpectedly resigned. He said he had been offered a job with a major corporation and that he was taking it. The next day he was gone.

After that, my boss never troubled me again about not working on Sundays. Sales in my department never wavered. In fact, they went steadily up. Years later, after I had moved on from that job, my former boss saw me on the street and told me I had been one of the best employees he'd ever had.

Jesus said, "That night when you prayed, I heard your prayers and intervened on your behalf. I delivered you from being fired, just as I delivered Shadrach, Meshach and Abednego from the flames of the furnace centuries earlier. For I am the only One who can deliver from the fire. You showed faith and courage by your actions. You honoured me, and that was witnessed by others. You stood firm and did what was right in my sight. Your actions were a great example to your fellow workers, your employer and all who heard about it. You helped strengthen the faith of others by taking the stand that you did, which in turn helped them to stand against evil when they encountered it. You also set a good example for your wife and children. You did well, my son."

That was gratifying to hear. "Thank You, Lord," I said.

My angel turned to me and smiled. Some of the despair I had been feeling began to leave. Maybe it would be all right.

CHAPTER 23

KINDNESS

Be kind and compassionate to one another, forgiving each
other, just as in Christ, God forgave you.
—Ephesians 4:32 (NIV)

Some of my fear began to leave, but not all, for despair has a way of
hanging around just beneath the surface.

The next scene opened.

I recognized the man immediately. He was sleeping in his van covered
with coats and blankets. It was starting to get cold at night. He had worked
for my uncle for many years, but my uncle had fired him. I really didn't
know him very well, but I had met him on several occasions.

I called Ron to ask why he had fired the man.

"He stole from us. He's lazy. He deserves what he gets. If he's sleeping
in his van, then good. Maybe he'll learn. Don't help him."

"What did he steal?" I asked.

"What does it matter? He stole."

I later learned that he was accused of stealing a can of pop. It sounded
pretty minor to me. I felt sorry for him. The few times I had talked to him
I always enjoyed our conversations. I found out that after losing his job
he had been evicted from his apartment because he was unable to pay the
rent. And because he had been fired in the way he was, he did not qualify
for government benefits.

I decided to help him despite what Ron had said. My best friend was
renting out rooms in his house, and I knew he had one available. I went to

see him and asked if he would rent the room to him if I promised to pay the rent until he got back on his feet. He agreed.

So I saw him while he was in his van and told him the arrangement I had worked out. He agreed to it and moved into my friend's house. He ended up living there for the remaining years of my life.

Eventually Julie and I were able to hire him to help out with Stephen. Fred became the best respite worker we had ever had. He was very good with Stephen when my son was in a bad mood, and he always seemed available at the last minute.

Another scene opened.

Again, I recognized it. It was embedded in my memory. I don't know that I was ever more nervous in my life than I was on that morning. I had been called to testify in a court case. I knew the opposing lawyers were really going to grill me. I didn't want to do it, but I had no choice.

I hadn't slept all night. My mouth was dry.

I parked my car in the paid lot and walked the two blocks to the court building. I had prayed all during my drive and was continuing to do so as I walked. A homeless man was sitting on the sidewalk begging. My initial thought was to just walk by and ignore him. I had too much on my mind to interact with a beggar.

But he spoke. "Do you have any change, sir?"

Normally I would have just ignored him and kept on walking, but the fact that he had said sir caught my attention. "No, I don't," I said brusquely. "I'm in a hurry. I have to testify today, even though I really don't want to."

"Well, all right then," he said. "You have a good day. God will be with you."

I was moved by his words. "Let me check my wallet." I looked for change and managed to find a few quarters and dimes that I gave to him.

"God bless you," he said as I departed.

A peace came over me as I entered the courtroom. As I testified, it seemed that the words were being given to me from somewhere else. It was as if someone was there helping me. I couldn't believe some of the things I said. I had the opposing attorneys completely flustered. The judge even smiled at me on occasion.

Another scene emerged.

It had happened today, the day of my death.

Jesus showed me the elderly lady from church that I had taken the time to purchase the medications for. She had heard about my accident and was praying for me. She was fervently calling out to God to have mercy on my soul. It was heart-warming to hear.

Jesus looked at me. "In all three of these instances you were conflicted about doing good, but in the end, you decided to show kindness. The day that you went to court you were earnestly pouring out your heart to me as you drove, and as you walked to the courthouse, I sent an angel to comfort you. The homeless man you encountered that day was that angel. You initially did not want to interact with him, but eventually you changed your mind and showed him kindness. Then, when you testified in court, the Holy Spirit helped bring to mind the words you needed to speak."

He continued. "Earlier today you did not initially want to do what your wife requested. But then you changed your mind and bought the medication for the elderly lady from church. Today she ardently prayed to me for your soul. Your uncle did not want you to help the man in the van who stole from your business. But in kindness, you decided to help him. He too has prayed to me for you, and I am carefully considering these prayers on your behalf."

This was remarkable to me. I barely knew the elderly lady from church, and now she was pleading to Jesus on my behalf. Yes, I had taken the time to go and buy medication for her, but it seemed like such a small thing.

"The kindnesses you do to others, no matter how small they may seem, will always come back to help you, my son. By helping others, you are, in fact, helping yourself. Kindness is reciprocal. When you show it to others, it will in turn be shown to you. The opposite is also true. If you are not kind to others, you will often not be shown kindness."

His words made perfect sense, and I pondered them. There were times in my life when I had shown kindness to others, but too often I had been too preoccupied with other things. I now wished I had done it more often.

"Yes, Lord, I understand," I said.

I turned to my angel. "Were you the homeless man on the street that day?"

"No, it was a friend of mine."

Had I done enough? It didn't feel like it. But at least I had done some good in my life. Maybe there was hope for me yet.

CHAPTER 24

BELIEF

Then Jesus told him, "Because you have seen me, you have
believed; blessed are those who have not seen and yet have
believed."

—John 20:29 (NIV)

Fred had time to relax after he got Stephen to bed. It had been a difficult
day. It had started with Stephen being stubborn and difficult to deal
with and had gone downhill from there. Then had come the news of the
accident and the sudden death of his employer. Then being there with
Stephen as he was told about his dad's death and now looking after him
overnight. It had been a tough, tough day.

Johnny had been only a couple of years older than him. He too was
in his fifties. One of his brothers had already died and his sister had just
gotten a diagnosis of incurable cancer. How long, he thought, before the
grim reaper came for him too? Life seemed to be passing by swiftly, and it
seemed with each passing year it moved faster and faster. How long would
it be before others were talking about his death or attending his funeral?

No matter how much time he had left, two things had become
glaringly obvious. One was that there would be no getting out of it.
Everybody died. No matter how healthy they were or how well they looked
after themselves or how good their genetics were, every person on the
earth would eventually succumb to death. That was an absolute certainty.
The second was that it would be here quick, quicker than we could ever
imagine.

He remembered the words of an aged evangelist he once heard. When asked what had surprised him most about life, the evangelist had simply replied, "The brevity of it."

This life was short and full of trouble. Might as well enjoy as much as you can, he reasoned, and remember your ultimate destiny. He knew God existed and that one day he would be with him. He had tried to live his life in the faith, and he truly believed that one day the Lord would reward him. Although he had always been poor in this life, he believed the true riches would come in the next one.

He believed that his employer would go to heaven. He'd had a few conversations with Johnny regarding his faith, and he believed that he was a true believer. He had said a prayer for his soul when he had heard about the accident.

He tried to relax and unwind with his favourite drink and some food. Thoughts about life and the deeper things possessed his mind. He needed to do as much good as he could in the days he had remaining. That would be his goal. Nothing else seemed to matter.

As he said his bedtime prayer, those thoughts predominated. "Use me, Lord, in whatever way you see fit."

He was willing and he believed that God would do it. About that he had no lack of confidence.

CHAPTER 25

FIDELITY

Watch over your heart with all diligence, for from it flow the springs of life.

—Proverbs 4:23 (NASB)

Another two prayers arrived for Jesus on my behalf. It made me feel better that people were praying for me. Although they couldn't know where I was or what I was doing, they prayed for my well-being. It helped.

The next scene opened.

She was a beautiful blonde who I had been working with for nearly a year. We were sitting in the breakroom at the same table having lunch.

"You know I really liked the last place I was working up north," she said. "I think I want to go back."

"Ya, why is that?" I asked.

"I don't know. I just like the people and the serenity, I guess."

Then she said something that really surprised me. "You should come with me."

That came as quite a shock. I liked this very attractive woman, but I had never thought about her in that way. I was in my first marriage at that time, and we were having difficulty, but running away with someone else was not something I had ever considered. It went against my values.

"I don't think my wife would like that," I said.

She responded quickly. "From what I hear, I don't think it would bother her too much."

I thought about that. Yes, things were rough between Lindsey and me, but I wasn't going to leave her and run off with another woman.

"I'm flattered," I said, "but I'm not leaving my wife."

Again, she responded quickly. "Well, if you ever change your mind, just let me know."

Time passed. I continued to work with her periodically and grew more and more attracted to her. My marriage continued to disintegrate. It appeared divorce was inevitable. Then I learned the beautiful woman's divorce had been finalized.

She approached me in the hallway one day. "You're beautiful," she said.

I looked at her with surprise.

"No, really. You are," she continued.

I didn't know what to say. The words she spoke came from a place of authenticity and struck deep within me. Lindsey had never said something like that to me even when times were good. In fact, no one had ever spoken to me like that before.

Temptation entered my mind. Sex had become a thing of the past in my marriage, but I saw that it wouldn't be a problem if I went with this woman. Desire was wooing me to break my marriage vows and start a new life with someone else.

I wrestled with it for weeks. Over and over, I fantasized about what it would be like to be with her and to no longer be married to my wife.

Then one day when I was visiting I overheard a conversation at my parents' house—a conversation I had heard many times before. My dad was telling my mom that maybe he should get a different woman.

"Go ahead," my mom replied. "Go get another woman. But just know that if you do, both you and she are gonna be dead. You can count on that."

My mom kept a twelve-gauge shotgun in the closet, and she was a pretty good shot. We all knew she didn't say things she didn't mean.

She continued. "And if any of my sons ever do that, they are no longer my son. I don't want to have anything to do with them."

My mom was like a brick wall on this subject. There was no alternative in her world. You did not cheat on your spouse. After hearing her I had clarity. I had made a vow. I had made a commitment. Keeping my word had always been important to me—one of my highest values. I wasn't going to change that now. I wouldn't be able to live with myself if I did.

So I remained faithful to my wife. The beautiful blonde woman completed her divorce and quit her job. I heard she moved back up north. I never saw her again.

Jesus said, "Just as you had tempted another earlier in your life, this woman tempted you. But you chose wisely and did not give in to the temptation. Because you could not be persuaded to leave your marriage, you provided her with an example of integrity and fidelity. She then had to consider what she was doing in her own life. You also provided an example for your children, for if you had given in to your desires, you would have badly damaged your relationships with them."

His words were a calming salve. I was humbled to hear them from my Creator.

He continued. "Faithfulness to my law will always produce blessings. Because you were faithful in this instance, you reaped blessings for the remainder of your life. Being unfaithful to my law, on the other hand, will always produce curses. You would have suffered the unpleasant consequences of your actions if you had given into temptation."

"Thank you, Lord," I said softly.

"Remain standing," Jesus said. "Your life review is nearly complete. Then a decision will be rendered as to where you will go next."

I was beginning to feel better about things. Hope grew within me. I had remained faithful to Lindsey throughout our twelve-year marriage. But I didn't know if that counted for much with her.

I stood taller beside my angel waiting for the next scene to open before me.

C H A P T E R 2 6

UNBELIEF

Take care, brothers and sisters, that none of you may have an evil, unbelieving heart that turns away from the living God.

—Hebrews 3:12 (NRSV)

It was now near midnight on the day of my death. Lindsey had calmed Keith down, reassuring him that his dad's death could not have been prevented by anything he did or did not do. Now she needed to calm herself and take stock of the day. She prepared her favourite treat to go with her favourite alcoholic beverage as she sat in her favourite recliner.

If ever there was a day that she deserved to overeat or drink, it was today. She was stunned by the turn of events. Johnny had always been in good health—better health than her—and her expectation had always been that he would outlive her. She counted on the child support he sent every month, and now that was gone. Keith was a voracious spender, and the best way to control his moods seemed to be by spending money on him. Johnny normally took care of that. She simply didn't have the funds.

She picked up her phone and called her sister, who was shocked to hear the news. But after calming herself down, she was unsympathetic toward her ex-brother-in-law.

"At least you won't have to deal with him anymore," she said. "He basically wrecked your life. You would have been better off if you had never met him. Divorcing you and then getting remarried before the ink was even dry on the divorce agreement. And then getting custody of the oldest kids. He was bad news for you."

"Yes, you're right," Lindsey said. "I'm not going to miss him, that's for sure. Johnny always thought he knew better than me when it came to the kids. He always had his nose in their business, trying to control everything. He always tried to tell everybody what to do, like he was the boss or something. Nobody's going to miss that. Anyway, the kids are all adults now except Keith. They can fend for themselves."

They continued talking for well over an hour.

"I suppose I should go the funeral," Lindsey said.

"Then you'll have to listen to all that religious nonsense again," her sister replied. "Just when you thought you had put all of that behind you, he gets you to go to church one last time. That's just like him."

"I know. Julie is super religious, so it's probably going to be super boring. But I guess I should go for the sake of the kids. It wouldn't look good if I didn't show up."

They continued talking about the ridiculousness of belief in God. Her sister was an atheist, and she had convinced Lindsey that Christianity was just a big fairy tale.

"I'll let Julie tell the grandchildren that he's in heaven. I'm not going to lie to them," Lindsey said.

After the call she snuggled down in her chair in front of the television. Johnny's death officially closed a chapter in her life that she would just as soon forget. He was gone now, and she would never have to deal with him again. She would never have to see his face or hear his voice or compromise on things regarding the kids. That was all over.

She would never have to listen to him talk about God or any of that church stuff anymore. With that comforting thought, she slowly fell asleep in her cosy recliner, the television blaring in front of her.

CHAPTER 27

GREED

Watch out! Be on your guard against all kinds of greed;
a man's life does not consist in the abundance of his
possessions.

—Luke 12:15 (NIV)

I was about to find out that Lindsey and her sister were not the only ones
who'd had an unfavourable opinion of me during my life.

Jesus showed me the next scene.

I saw myself writing out notices of rental increases to my tenants. In
my single years, as my income increased, I had bought inexpensive houses
and rented them out as a form of secondary income. I had five properties
that I rented out to low-income families. The rents they paid were quite
reasonable in my view, and I saw myself as being a good landlord.

One year, a natural gas find near our town caused an explosion in real
estate values. Many people moved to town for the high-paying jobs. There
was a shortage of housing, and home prices and rental prices skyrocketed.
At first I didn't react. I saw what was happening, but I really didn't think
it would affect me that much. At least that was until a real estate friend
and I were talking one day.

"Do you still have those rental properties?" he asked. I nodded. "Have
you raised your rents?"

"No. I hadn't really thought about it."

"You should. Everyone in town is raising their rents. There's a shortage of housing, and that's driving up prices. I've raised the rents on all my properties by thirty percent."

That sounded like a lot to me. "Is that legal?"

"No law against it," he replied.

I thought about what he said. I was living a comfortable life and really didn't need the extra money. *But,* I thought, *this might be a great opportunity to put some money away for a rainy day.* I checked out the government guidelines and found out that my friend was indeed correct. It was completely legal. So I started the process of raising the rents.

Of course, that wasn't popular with my tenants. But I reasoned that if they didn't like it, they were free to move somewhere else. That wasn't really an option, though, with the suddenly tight real estate market in town. I figured that compared to others, they were still getting a good deal renting with me. So I slept well at night. I still viewed myself as a good guy. Yes, I had raised rents by quite a bit, but I heard of many others who had raised them by much more.

Another scene opened before me.

It was a few months later. It was inside the house of one of my properties. There was little food in the cupboards or the fridge. The children looked thin and wore tattered clothing. The husband and wife sat talking at the kitchen table. They were talking about me.

"We don't have enough money to pay all our bills," the wife said. "Ever since that landlord raised the rent so much higher, we don't even have enough for food."

The husband concurred. "I know. Prices of everything in town have gone up, but my wages stay the same. I don't know what to do."

I winced as I viewed the scene. I hadn't considered the pressure I was putting on my tenants by raising the rents so much. I was only focused on the numbers in my bank account. Those numbers kept going up and up. That gave me a great deal of satisfaction. I started to have dreams of becoming rich. A few times, the tenants asked about a rent decrease or to delay payment, but I always politely refused. I was getting used to my new lifestyle. I bought a new truck because I could now easily afford the payments. I went on an exotic holiday and enjoyed relaxing on the beach and staying in a nice hotel.

The problem I now saw, however, was that my tenants struggled to put food on the table. I heard of one couple who were using the food bank. One day I saw one of my tenants scouring garbage cans for bottles. Another moved to another town, and I heard that he and his family had to move in with his brother, which had caused a lot of difficulty. At the time, these things never resonated with me.

Eventually the real estate boom dissipated. I moved on with my life and sold all my rental properties after I married. I never once felt bad about what I had done. I never felt a scintilla of guilt for my actions. After all, I thought, I had not done anything wrong. Everything I had done was perfectly legal. That was my thinking. At least until now.

I glanced at Jesus, unable to look fully at him.

"What do you say about your actions, my son?"

I didn't know what to say. It was so obvious viewing the events from this vantage point that I had been captivated by greed. I had padded my bank account at the expense of others with money I didn't need. I had lived a lifestyle of ease and comfort while others barely managed to get by. I had felt no compassion for those who were suffering because of my selfishness.

"I don't know what to say, Lord. I see now that I was being greedy. I am without excuse," I whispered.

"You rationalized your actions because others were doing the same thing, sometimes even worse than you. You felt justified because you compared yourself with others. It was not a wise thing to do. Just because others were committing sin did not excuse you for doing it. You felt that because you were obeying man's law, you were all right. But you failed to see that you were breaking my law, to treat others as you would like to be treated. You became intoxicated with the lifestyle your actions produced, and thus you became blinded to the suffering you were imposing on others, even though they asked you for mercy."

I listened as he spoke, my eyes cast downward. "I was wrong, Lord," I finally said.

I had been a fool. I had become enamoured with my bank account and had completely ignored the hardships of my tenants. Why had I not seen? Why had I been so caught up with greed? This surely was the final straw. How could I go to heaven after this? Thoughts spun through my head. I did not want to go to hell. What would happen to me? I slumped to my knees.

I remembered the story of Lazarus and the rich man in the Bible. I now saw that I was the rich man and that my tenants were Lazarus. And I remembered what had happened to the rich man. He had gone to the place of torment. I sat there staring blindly ahead.

My angel approached and tried to comfort me. "You made a mistake," he said, "but that mistake does not define who you are. There is still more of your life review to see. You must watch it."

And who was I really? Did I truly even know who I was? I was speechless. Numbness overtook me. Defeat closed in around me.

CHAPTER 28

DEFEAT

The Lord is close to the brokenhearted and saves those
who are crushed in spirit.

—Psalm 34:18 (NIV)

I felt crushed. My angel and I sat together in silence for a long while.

"I never realized who I was when I was alive," I finally said. "I mean,
who I really was."

I paused for a moment. "I barely recognize the person I see in this life
review at times. I see the images and know it's me, and I remember when
a lot of these things happened. But I didn't realize what my actions were
really doing. I always thought I was a good person. I didn't commit any
major crimes or kill anybody or steal from people. I obeyed the law, except
for speeding sometimes or fudging my income taxes once in a while.

"But now I see how wrong my thinking was in other areas. I was always
in a hurry to accomplish what I wanted to accomplish. I rushed from one
thing to the next. I should have slowed down and seen life more from the
point of view of other people I encountered. I should have seen it more
from God's point of view. But I didn't. And now it's too late."

My angel listened patiently. He did not immediately speak. He
appeared distracted by something.

After a moment he finally said, "It may not be too late. I do not know
what will happen next, but I do know the Lord is very merciful. I also
know there are events in your life that have not been shown to you yet."

I pondered his words. "Well, I don't know what those events would be," I replied, "and he did say it was nearly over. Does it really matter? My life is over and it's too late to go back and change it. I now see that I wasn't really truly successful at anything. I'm not who I thought I was."

I sat slouched over.

Jesus spoke. "My son, your true life does not consist of what you did or did not accomplish. I do not reward souls for the successful fulfilment of their work but rather for the sincere will and desire to undertake it. I look at the motivations of the heart. I consider the talents you were given and how you made use of them or did not make use of them. My judgment is not like man's judgment."

I heard what he said, but I wasn't sure I completely understood. And I didn't know how it applied to me.

He spoke with kindness. "It is now time to complete your life review. Stand and watch, because your knowledge of who you really are is not yet complete."

"Yes Lord," I said.

I slowly got up and raised my head. My angel did the same, shaking his wings gently as he stood. I just wanted it to be over, but I had no power to end it. I waited for the next scene to open.

CHAPTER 29

UNFAIRNESS

This is why I weep and my eyes overflow with tears. No one is near to comfort me, no one to restore my spirit.

—Lamentations 1:16 (NIV)

My teenage son had cried most of the night, unable to fall asleep. Everything seemed so unfair. His dad was dead. A pillar in his unstable life was now gone. And he was heartbroken.

Keith believed his mom and girlfriend that there was nothing he could have done to prevent the accident. He knew his dad was a good driver, but he had noticed that as he was getting older, he was making the odd mistake. It wasn't hard to believe that his dad had just been a bit distracted by something and had accidently pulled out in front of a truck. He could envision that happening. But that didn't make accepting what had happened any easier. He couldn't stop crying. He couldn't stop wondering why his life was the way it was. He didn't understand. It just didn't make any sense.

He thought about killing himself sometimes. That would end the pain. But that wouldn't bring his dad back. Nothing was going to bring his dad back. He knew that. When he was younger, he had gone into his grandmother's living room and found her sitting in her chair. She was dead. That incident had caused him trauma that he still had not fully recovered from. His dad had been there that day. He had seen how hard his dad had taken his mother's death. He never thought that just a few years later his dad would be the one who died.

It just wasn't right. It wasn't fair. His friends' parents and grandparents were all still alive. Why would he lose both his grandmother and his dad—two people in the world he really loved and he knew really loved him? A deep sadness filled him. It was deeper than any sadness he had ever felt before. He didn't know if he would ever get over it. He would have to live his life without his dad. He was the one who came to all his games and made sure he had the best equipment. He was the one who dealt with his teachers at school and made sure they treated him fairly. He was the one who was always there when he got into trouble and needed someone to come, which with his fetal alcohol syndrome was a frequent occurrence. He knew he could always count on his dad—day or night, winter or summer. If he needed him, he was always just a phone call away.

And now he was gone—gone forever. He just wanted to punch something. He wanted to punch something so hard that it shattered into a thousand pieces. He wanted to shatter something the way he felt shattered.

He started punching his mattress harder and harder and harder. "Why, why, why?" he cried.

He stopped punching and rolled into the bed and buried his head under the pillow.

No answer came. He wept. Life was so hard. It was too hard. It just wasn't fair.

CHAPTER 30

LOVE

And now these three remain: faith, hope, and love. But
the greatest of these is love.

—1 Corinthians 13:13 (NIV)

My life review sped up. Scene after scene rapidly played out before me. I
saw my family life from the time of my youth into adulthood. Over and
over, I saw scenes between me and other family members of both love and
conflict. I saw that as my life passed and I grew older, the scenes of conflict
decreased and the scenes of love increased.

I also saw the scenes of love and conflict that I had with others who
were not in my family. It seemed to be the same. As I aged, I seemed to
have more patience with people and less contention. That's not to say I
necessarily became less grumpy, but I seemed to be better able to control
my negative emotions and my tongue.

I saw scene after scene of actions I had taken, both good and bad. I
saw how my actions affected the lives of those around me and how even
seemingly small things could cause either a positive or negative effect in
people's lives. It seemed that every action I took, every word I spoke had
meaning. In the drama that was my life, it seemed there had been few
random repercussions. My life had been completely interlocked with the
lives of those I was in contact with, and my actions and words directly
affected theirs. I saw how my stubbornness and unwillingness to change
could hurt other people and how my narrow focus on what I wanted
often caused me to be unaware of their feelings. I saw that when I showed

patience and forgiveness it benefited others, and to this there seemed to be no exceptions.

It occurred to me that most of the scenes involved my family. I saw the pain, joy, sorrow and love that surrounded me. I saw how important my role was in the family. I saw that the overriding thing that held it all together was love. When love was missing, it seemed that things came undone. But when it was there, it was like a glue that forged an unbreakable bond between people. It seemed to be the most powerful force in the universe. It was fascinating to watch.

Then the scenes stopped, and Jesus spoke.

"It was in the crucible of the family that you learned to love and deal with conflict. In families, you must interact with those that you might otherwise ignore. But you cannot ignore them if they are in your family, although at times you might try. In this way you learn to see the points of view of others, and you learn to love others even when they have a viewpoint that is different from your own. You grew in this during your lifetime. You were not perfect, but as your life progressed you became better and better."

His words were consoling. They infiltrated me to my core.

"As you grew older you had more patience with those you did not like, and you tolerated others better with whom you had strong disagreements. You learned this primarily in your family, and then you practiced it with people in general. You showed love to others as you learned to be more patient and forgiving, even when you disagreed with them. For love is not only shown when you give it to those with whom you like and agree with. It is often best shown when you exhibit it toward those who are different from you and with whom you do not agree. You matured in this as your life went along and it was obvious that had you lived longer you would have continued to do so. You slowly began to learn that feeling hatred toward others did not bring you the peace you desired. This was pleasing to me, my son."

I did not know what to say. This was such a sharp contrast from the scenes I had just witnessed about my greed.

"Thank you, Lord, for showing me this. I deeply appreciate it."

"You will now see more scenes from your life right up until the time of your death. Observe them carefully, for they will help you better understand who you really are and who you need to become."

"Yes, Lord," I said.

But I didn't fully understand what he was talking about. What did he mean by "who you need to become"? Was there still a way for me to change, even after my death? Was it still not too late? I couldn't fathom it. But I continued to watch.

Scenes now passed with great speed right up to the accident and my death. They seemed to speed by quicker and quicker as I grew older. And then it came to an end. My life review was over. I knew that my eternal fate would now be determined.

CHAPTER 31

EVERY IDLE WORD

But I say unto you that for every idle word men may speak, they will give account of it in the day of judgment. For by your words you will be justified, and by your words you will be condemned.

—Matthew 12:36–37 (NKJV)

It wasn't over though. Not quite yet.

Jesus spoke. "Now you must give an account for the words you have spoken, my son. You will be shown many instances of the things that you said during your life, both good and bad. You must give an explanation for saying the things you said. You must also give your motivation for saying them, for often it is not what is said that is most important but rather the reason the words were spoken and the tone in which they were said. Watch and listen carefully."

I wasn't sure I was ready for this. In fact, I knew I wasn't. I knew that I had said many things in my life that I had regretted later. I also knew that most of the time I had never apologized for my words. I had said some positive things, yes, but I was worried about the negative ones.

The scenes went by again.

The words that I had spoken in bitterness and anger were graphically portrayed before me. It seemed that every insult, every name calling, every time I used bad language, every bad word that I had ever spoken was shown to me.

On and on it went, bitter words sometimes laced with profanity. As

I watched, I realized I'd had no idea how much vitriol had poured out of my mouth over the years. My words were sharp and harsh, and for the first time I heard them coming out of my mouth as others had heard them. I was good at articulating an insult and hurling it with force at my victim. And I had done it time and time again. It wasn't pleasant to watch and listen to.

I cringed. I winced. I cowered. I flinched. I was aghast, alarmed and horrified at times by the things I had said, the tone I had used and the obvious motivation behind the words. Often my intent was to hurt and injure.

"What do you say about this?" Jesus asked.

What could I say? I had never really understood the deep-seated effect my words had had until now. I had been cruel and unfeeling. I had no excuse. My words had lived on down to this very moment ringing through the corridors of time. It had never once occurred to me that I would have to one day give an account for the words I had spoken, even those spoken decades before.

"What *can* I say? I see how offensive and hateful I was. I should have been more careful with what I said and how I said it. I am really sorry for all of those whom I have hurt." My face was cast downward.

He said, "The tongue can be a source of death or a source of life depending on how it is used. If it is used as a weapon to inflict pain, it is a source of death. The words you spoke welled up from inside your heart and spilled out of your mouth on to others. Words spoken in anger and bitterness can become imprinted on the minds of others, and sometimes they must carry that burden with them the rest of their lives. Most often those words are never apologized for, and thus the balm of remorse is never applied to the wound that was inflicted. This is a burden you placed on some during your life."

I knew it was true. I could not deny it. How I wished I could go back and apologize to each individual I had wounded and spoken unkindly to. How I wished I could apply the balm of remorse to the wounds I had inflicted. But it was too late. Now I would face the consequences of my words. I continued to hang my head.

"Lift up your head," Jesus said, "and watch the remainder."

I didn't want to, but I did.

My angel put his hand on my shoulder. That was a comfort. "It will be all right," he said. "You'll see."

I didn't know how he could possibly know that, but at least he made me feel somewhat better. More scenes opened, one after another. This time, however, they were different. They were positive instead of negative.

"You're a great guy. Well done. That was beautiful. Thank you so much. You're wonderful. You're the best. She's awesome. You were so kind. I really appreciate that. I love you."

Again, on and on it went. It was beautiful. Beneficial and loving words poured from my mouth like clear streams of water. I'd had no idea how many positive things I had said during my lifetime. It was refreshing—a wellspring of positivity. It felt good to see and hear.

Jesus again spoke. "You see that you also had a very good effect on others with your words. Those positive words can also be imprinted on the minds of others and genuinely influence their lives for the better. They often stay with them the remainder of their lives. You did this many times in your life."

I felt better. Again, my angel put his hand on my shoulder. He looked at me and smiled.

"Now you must see the most important words that you spoke during your life," Jesus said. "Stand and watch."

I was now shown the words that I had spoken about the Father, Son and Holy Spirit. I saw scene after scene of what seemed like everything I had ever said about them and what I believed about them. I saw and heard the many times I had told others that I believed in them and that I believed Jesus had died for me. I saw the many prayers of repentance I had said asking for God's forgiveness for my sins. I saw the times of doubt when I struggled with my faith. I saw the times I confessed my faith publicly before others. I saw the times I was sure God was intervening in my life and the times when it felt like he had left me.

But one common strand ran through it all—that I had always believed even when that belief had been weak.

Jesus said, "My son, you spoke of your belief in me throughout most of your life. Although your faith was not always strong and you did not always speak when opportunities arose, you nevertheless always believed that I died for you on that cross outside Jerusalem almost two thousand years before. You desired forgiveness for your sins although you did not always recognize them. You asked me to forgive you, and I did. I suffered and died for you that day and I carried all your sins with me as I was nailed to that cross. My shed blood covered all your sins, for I knew you even then, even before you were born. The scourging I took, the whipping, the mocking and the beatings—all of that I did for you. And you accepted what I did and believed in my name."

He looked straight at me, and it was as if he could see right through me. I was mesmerized.

"I have examined your heart, my son. I have looked closely at your words, thoughts and actions. I heard what you said about the things you have been shown. I have taken into account all your strengths and weaknesses, abilities and disabilities, talents and limitations, faith and doubts. I have considered the prayers that have been offered up on your behalf. I am now ready to render my judgment."

My throat constricted. I was without breath. I was paralyzed. I closed my eyes.

Jesus said, "I now say to you as I said to that thief that was on the cross beside me that day, 'You will be with me in paradise.' Well done, my son."

Had I heard him right? Did he say I would be with him in paradise? That meant I was going to go to heaven! I was stunned. The enormity of the words Jesus had just spoken to me left me numb and speechless.

And then I wasn't. "Thank you, Lord! Thank you, thank you, thank you, a million times thank you!" I shouted, filled with euphoria. "I will praise and love you forever!"

Overwhelming joy and jubilation swept over me. It was over. I was so full of emotion that I didn't know what to do. All the fears and doubts and guilt and rejections of the past melted away and disappeared. Relief overcame me. I was going to heaven!

I turned to my angel and gave him the biggest bear hug I had ever given. "I'm going to heaven! Thank you for being with me all my life and especially today, when things looked bad. I'm sorry for all the times I caused you trouble."

He smiled broadly as I released him from my grip.

"It was no trouble," he replied. "It was my duty, and I was happy to do it. Congratulations."

Jesus allowed me time to take in what had just happened. I cried tears of joy. I danced with my angel even though I had never been a dancer. I sat and thought about the wonder of it all. But most of all, I just praised Jesus.

The Lord spoke again. "You will go to heaven, my son, but first you must be purified from the stain of sin that remains on your soul. You must be cleansed of the unforgiveness, the greed, the lust, the sloth, the pride, the envy, the wrath, the gluttony and the lack of remorse that still clings to you. For no soul that has impurities may live in heaven with me. You must be perfect as your heavenly Father is perfect before you go before him. No uncleanness can be allowed in heaven. Now you will go to a place of purification to be cleansed of these and other blemishes so you can be made ready for heaven. After you have been cleansed, you will be allowed to put on the garments of heaven that you must be wearing before you enter there. You will be taken to the level appropriate for you based on the judgment you have just received. Your angel will escort you there now."

I had never heard of this place of purification. I didn't know that such a place existed. I had always thought that when a person died, they either went straight to heaven or hell. I did not know of a place where one could be cleansed from the remaining stains of sin on one's soul.

"Come with me," my angel said.

I turned to Jesus again. "Thank you, Lord. I will never be able to thank you enough. Thank you for suffering for me to make this possible. I love you," I said.

"I know you do. And now you must suffer for a little while so that we may be together forever in my Father's house. I love you, my son," He said.

Those were the most precious words I had ever heard. All the pains and trials and sufferings of life now seemed to be worth it. All fear and anxiety seemed to completely vanish. A complete and total peace permeated me. I felt like a new person, even though I was still the same being I had been when my accident occurred seemingly not that long before.

The difference was that now at last I felt that I knew who I really was. I felt transparent. There was no longer any need to hide my true self from others or wear a mask. I now knew who I was and what I needed to change in order to become who I needed to become.

My angel led me away. It had been quite a day. But it wasn't over yet. The next step of my journey was about to begin.

CHAPTER 32

MY ANGELIC ESCORT

Are not all angels ministering spirts sent to serve those
who will inherit salvation?

—Hebrews 1:14 (NIV)

We flew away from the presence of Jesus. I did not know how long it
would take to get to this place of purification or where it was, but I was
unconcerned. My entire being was filled with unspeakable peace and joy.
I knew for certain that my salvation was assured and that I was going to
live with Jesus in heaven. That was all that mattered.

I actually wanted to go to this place of purification. I had seen the ugly
uncleanness that was still on my soul during the life review, uncleanness
that I had never dealt with during my life. I felt bad about it and now
desired more than anything to remove it. I longed to have no more
blemishes on my soul so that I could be worthy to wear the garments of
heaven. I desired to be perfect as Jesus was perfect.

Jesus had said that I must suffer there. I asked my angel about
that. "What did Jesus mean when he said I must suffer in this place of
purification?"

"You must suffer in order to remove the taint of sin that remains on
your soul," he replied. "Jesus suffered and shed His blood so that your
sins could be forgiven. And so, they are. But you still have stains and
blemishes on your soul. The suffering you will experience there will remove
those stains and blemishes and help to purify you. There is great value in
suffering. All humans who wish to go to heaven must suffer before they

go there, either in their earthly life or in the place of purification or both. There are no exceptions. You cannot become who you need to become without it."

I pondered that. I had always viewed suffering as a negative thing in my life—a kind of punishment for wrongdoing. But I now understood that that wasn't necessarily the case. It was starting to make sense.

"Do angels suffer?" I asked.

My angel nodded. "We only suffer if we refuse to obey the Father. We, like you, have free will. Some of my fellow spirits decided they did not want to obey the Father. They rebelled and were removed from heaven. Most are now on the earth. Humans call them demons. They suffer—and will continue to suffer—because of their decision to rebel. They attempt to influence humans to join them and suffer with them in hell—their ultimate destination."

"Wow," I said. "So there really are demons?"

"Oh yes," my angel replied, "and many humans don't even believe in them. That's the way they want it because it makes humans easier to deceive with their schemes. We encounter them a lot when we are on the earth. But Jesus's name will repel them. They hate it, just as they hate the humans who wish to be saved and live in heaven—the place they were removed from and can never go back to. If they cannot go to heaven, then they want no one else to go there either."

This was so interesting. I had heard of evil spirits, but I never really believed in them. I saw now that they were there the entire time trying to sway me.

My angel continued. "Those of us who choose to obey the Father do not suffer as humans do. Because we do not suffer as you do, we also cannot attain what you can, which is to be joined as one with Jesus. You can be joined with Jesus through suffering. We cannot do that. For you it is a great honour."

I thought about what he said. I had never heard it put like that before. I had never considered it an honour to suffer. But Jesus had suffered. There must be honour in it. There was no envy or jealousy in the angel's voice. He seemed content with his role in the scheme of things. He simply gave me straightforward answers to my questions.

"Will you stay with me in this place of purification?"

"No, I will not be staying with you there as you do not require a guardian angel while you are there. I will visit you at times to let you know how your friends and relatives on the earth are doing. Soon I will be given other duties, as my assignment with you is nearly completed."

I reflected on his words. This angel had been my lifelong companion, and I never even knew he was there. Now that I had spent time with him and could see and talk with him, I very much liked him.

"Well, I hope I wasn't too difficult for you," I said.

"You weren't—but you had your moments. Three times during your life I had to intervene to prevent you from dying before your appointed time. Once when you nearly got swept into the ocean by a wave, once when you almost pulled out in front of a car and once when you were young and fell out of a tree. I had to alter all three of those events or you most certainly would have died before today."

I remembered all three of those incidents. I remembered thinking each time that I had been lucky. Now I realized my survival had not been a matter of luck.

"Thank you for doing that for me," I said. In my naivete I added, "Maybe I can help you sometime."

My angel merely smiled at that.

We were approaching a place of grey clouds and dim light.

"This is the place of purification," my angel said. "I will take you to where you have been assigned to go, but first I have been instructed to make a stop so you can see someone."

We entered, and I saw why Jesus had said I would suffer. I was already beginning to feel it. The moment we arrived I felt discomfort and pain building within me.

We went to a gate that led to a level. There was a man standing there who looked like he was waiting for someone. As we drew closer, recognition came to my mind. Was this who I thought it was? Surely it was. I ran toward him.

CHAPTER 33

REUNION

> While he was still a long way off his father saw him and
> was filled with compassion for him; he ran to his son,
> threw his arms around him and kissed him.
>
> —Luke 15:20 (NIV)

As I came closer, there was no longer any doubt. It was my dad.

He ran toward me, and we embraced. It had been a long while since I had seen him. He had died fifteen years before my death.

"Hello, Johnny! It's so good to see you!" he said, tears in his eyes. "My guardian angel told me you were coming. He obtained permission for us to meet."

"It's so good to see you again, Dad!" I said, hugging him for a long time. "I just finished my life review, and Jesus said I would go to heaven! But he said I would have to spend some time here first. I had no idea I would see you here!"

My dad looked much younger than the last time I had seen him, but I could see pain and sorrow etched on his face. "Did you see your mom?"

"Yes," I said. "I saw her just before my life review. She was so happy and joyful. She was radiant. I've never seen her look so good. She wasn't down or preoccupied like she used to be when we were alive. She said you were somewhere else, but I didn't know it was here."

"I'm glad you saw her. I haven't seen her for quite some time. After she died, she was here for a brief while and I was able to see her a few times. But she was soon able to go to heaven, and since then I haven't seen her.

She doesn't visit this place of suffering. I long to go to heaven and see her again, but it will probably be a long time before I do."

I looked at him, perplexed. "Why do you say that, Dad? And why was Mom only here for a short time? I don't understand."

He paused for a moment. "I was not the best of people during my life. They say some people have a special gift when it comes to tormenting others, and I had that gift. I used it to torment your mom the many years we were married. I used it on others, of course, but your mom bore the brunt of my unkindness. You probably didn't see much of it because I was rarely that way around you or my friends. It was only those I didn't like or I felt needed correcting that I victimized. I felt inferior to your mom, so I criticized her virtually every day to make myself feel better. I could always find something wrong with what she was doing or what she said or didn't say. No matter how small a thing was, I could always find a way to turn it into a much bigger issue than it was. I made everything her fault. If there was a problem in our marriage, which in my view there always was, I could always find a way to put the blame on her. I could always twist her words and use them against her no matter what she said. I was a master at it."

I listened intently. This was a revelation to me.

"Over the years she just grew silent when I criticized her. She stopped talking back. I redoubled my efforts and criticized her even more, but it didn't work. I exaggerated any tiny flaws she may have had and even made things up. But eventually it seemed to have little effect on her. Why she didn't divorce me I don't know. It had to have been because of her strong faith."

My mom had always talked of her faith, even though she had not been raised in a Christian home.

"Finally, when I realized I was dying, I asked God for forgiveness for the way I had acted. On my deathbed I apologized to your mom. Jesus did forgive me, but after my life review he said I would have to spend much time in this place of purification because I had badly tarnished my soul by my words and actions during my life. I was actually overjoyed about that because as I watched my life review, I thought I would certainly go to hell. Jesus was very merciful."

He paused for a moment. A tear came to his eye. He collected himself and continued.

"During my life review, I saw that your mom had prayed for me every day we were together and that every day she had asked God to forgive me for the mean things I had said to her. She is a good woman. I shudder to think what might have happened to me without her prayers. I deserve to be here, and be here for a long time, and she deserves to be in heaven. She was here for only a short time because of the patience she showed as she endured my cruelty. She did most of her suffering during her lifetime. One day I will go to heaven, but that time is a long way off, I imagine."

I was startled to hear this. I had on occasion seen my dad say things to my mom that seemed harsh, but that was rare. I really had no idea what their relationship had really been like.

"Why weren't you that way toward me?" I asked. "I don't remember you being like that."

"You were my favourite," he said. "I favoured you over your brothers and sisters. I always treated you better than anyone else in the family, maybe because you reminded me of myself. The others saw it, but maybe you didn't. No matter what you said or did, I almost always went easy on you and was tougher on your siblings. That's another reason I must spend a long time here."

I was astonished. At times I had kind of thought that was the case, but as a kid I always thought my brothers and sisters were just getting what they deserved. After all, I reasoned, they just weren't being as good as me.

"I didn't know." I said.

As we sat talking, discomfort crept into me until it become outright pain. It was dreary here and the light was dim.

"Are you suffering much?" I asked him.

"Oh, yes," he responded quickly. "I'm suffering terrible pain even as we are talking here. I have suffered ever since I arrived, and I don't know how long that's been since time has little meaning here. The flames are excruciatingly painful at times. But I know I deserve it and that I will go to heaven eventually. That makes it all bearable. I have completed a few circles and moved up levels since I've been here, but I'm still a ways away from cleansing the stains on my soul."

"Is there any way to relieve the suffering, even for a while?" I asked.

"There is a way," he responded, "and that is when those still on the earth pray for us here. Unfortunately, no one on the earth is actively praying for me. I don't know if that is because I was so disagreeable during my life, or they just don't realize they could help. The only ones praying for me are your mom and those in heaven who know I'm here."

The pain I felt was becoming more severe. I felt it was time to move on.

"Will I see you again?" I asked.

"Yes. We can meet periodically. We will be in different areas, but there will be opportunities to see each other if the Lord permits. If you can, please visit me before you go to heaven," he begged.

I wasn't sure I would be going to heaven before him, but I promised I would. "I will for sure, Dad. I love you."

"I love you, son. I'm sorry I didn't tell you that during our lifetimes."

That meant a lot to me. My dad had never told me he loved me. I always felt that he did, but he never actually said it.

I turned to my angel. "I guess it's time to go."

"All right," he replied, "if you're sure. I know how special the parent-child relationship is. It is a great gift from the Father to humans."

I hadn't thought about it that way before, but he was right. "I'm sure," I said.

He then led me away to my level. I was now feeling extremely uncomfortable and in outright pain. Despite that, though, there was an underlying sense of joy and peace in my being. I felt I could endure anything now. I was going to go to heaven to live with Jesus. He had told me that himself. It was only a matter of time.

PURGATORY

There is going to come a time of testing at Christ's
Judgment Day to see what kind of material each builder
has used. Everyone's work will be put through the fire so
that all can see whether or not it keeps its value, and what
was really accomplished.

—1 Corinthians 3:13 (CLB)

I entered the place of purification. It was dull and cloudy, and the light
was a misty half-darkness. It felt like flames entered my body and afflicted
me. And then they became visible. I saw them lapping at me. I tried to
walk away from them, but they followed me wherever I went. They pierced
me but were tolerable—barely. I then saw others moving around in what
looked like prayer and contemplation.

My angel spoke. "This place is divided into levels and circles. This is
the level and circle I was instructed to bring you to. I will be leaving you
now. You will meet others here who will explain more about this place."

"When will I see you again?"

"I will visit you when I can."

"Thank you," I said. "You truly have been a wonderful guardian for
me. I truly appreciate what you have done."

"It was my pleasure," my angel replied and left.

I moved further in to where the others were. There were many souls
here, many more than what I could have imagined. I saw a woman coming
toward me who I recognized immediately. She had worked with me twenty

years previously, and we'd had many good conversations. She looked much like she had when we worked together except for the painful expression on her face.

"Johnny! I heard you were coming, and I wanted to greet you," she said cheerfully. "I'm happy to see you again!"

"Wow!" I said. "I can't believe it's you! You look good. This seems so strange. I was just at your funeral a few months ago. I never, ever thought I'd be seeing you again so soon!"

"Nor I!" she replied as we embraced.

She had died of cancer a few months before my accident. I had attended her funeral, which was huge. She had been a well-known and well-liked member of the community.

"I stayed around for my funeral after I died," she said. "I remember seeing you there. Thank you for coming."

"That was no problem," I said. "I always liked you. I wanted to be there."

We looked at each other for a moment. We were both happy, but the burning pain was always present.

"This is new to me," I said. "I just arrived, and I don't know much about this place. My guardian angel said there would be others here who could explain things to me. I guess that means you, at least for now."

"Well, I guess it does," she replied with a grin. "This is the circle of longsuffering. Here we are cleansed of impatience, especially impatience with others, but also impatience with ourselves. I was not patient enough with others in my life, so now I must have that stain removed from my soul. The burning flames that you see and feel are the flames of purification. They burn away the impurities from us, leaving only what is pure. When we have been cleansed of this impatience we will move on to the next circle or level to be purified of whatever else we need to be cleansed of. When we are completely pure, we will be ready to go to heaven. Were you impatient during your life?"

That question struck at my inmost being. I had always been in a hurry, impatient for people and events to move faster. There was no doubt about it—I had been impatient during my life.

"Yes," I said. "In fact, if I hadn't been in such a hurry today, I might well have not died. I've always been impatient—especially with other people, I'm sorry to say."

"Well, that's why you're here then. You need to be cleansed of that before you can go to heaven."

A light came on in my mind. So that's what Jesus meant when he said I must become what I need to become. I need to be the person I am, but I need to get rid of my impurities. I did not do that during my life, so I would have to have it done here. I cannot enter heaven with them being part of my being. I had to be cleansed first. It was making sense.

"You don't really know where you are, do you?" She smiled.

I looked at her a bit confused. "Jesus told me this is the place of purification."

"Yes, that's true, but in my church we called it purgatory."

Now I remembered that in my conversations with her she had talked about being Catholic. I too was a churchgoer, so we'd had a few discussions about religion. I had vaguely heard of purgatory, but I never remembered talking about it with her. I knew my church did not believe that such a place existed. But as I was learning more and more, what I believed when I was alive was completely irrelevant now. If I had been an atheist, what relevance would that have had when I was standing in front of the God who created me? If I didn't believe in purgatory, what relevance would that have now that I was here? It did exist and I was in it.

"Well, your church was right about this," I said. "Obviously." I looked at the flames lapping up against me. "What else can you tell me about this place? I learned nothing about it during my lifetime."

She smiled at me again. "You know, I always enjoyed our conversations, even though I believed you were wrong about some things. You were always so sincere."

"So it is here that you must be purified of the remaining blemishes on your soul. God requires that we all be perfect before we can enter heaven. We would be out of place there if we weren't. The flames here remove imperfections. Do you remember in the Bible where it says that you must be holy or you won't be able to see the Lord? This is the place where that holiness is achieved if it is not accomplished during our lives. We saw the light around Jesus during our life reviews, but in heaven we will see him face to face. God loves us and he wants us to live with him in heaven forever. That is why the flames here are often referred to as the flames of God's love."

Wow, I thought, that really was logical. As it was, I didn't feel ready to go to heaven and be with God. After watching my life review, I felt dirty. I felt like I needed a good bath before I went before the King.

"Why are so many people praying?" I asked. "Are they praying to God to release them from this place?"

"No. We cannot directly pray for ourselves while we're here. We can pray for our family and friends and anyone else still on the earth. We can pray for those whom we sinned against and caused harm to during our lives. Our prayers can benefit them as we intercede for them. Just as you prayed for others when you were alive, you can still do that now."

"Wow, I never knew. How do we know what to pray about?"

"The guardian angels visit us and tell us how those that we knew on the earth are doing. Of course, people on the earth can pray for our help, and God makes their requests known to us."

This was incredible. I had never in my life imagined this. I wondered if anyone on the earth would pray for me or ask for my prayers for them. *Probably not,* I thought.

"How will others even know I'm here?" I asked. "None of my family or friends even believe in purgatory or know what it is."

"You can pray to God to reveal it to them. He might do that," she said. "Of course if people pray for you that can sometimes shorten your stay here. That, too, is possible."

That was astonishing to me. "You mean that people on the earth can pray for people in purgatory to shorten their stay? That's amazing."

"It's true. Some of my relatives and friends have been praying for me. It helps. It also helps alleviate some of the pain."

I knew no one would be praying for me. They didn't even know this place existed, let alone that I might be here.

I thanked her for the information and prayed for those I had left behind and those to whom I had caused harm. Praying here felt different. It felt more real and intense. I now knew God was listening to my prayers. There was no doubt he heard them. When I was alive, stray thoughts often entered while I prayed, but here I could stay totally focused on the one I was praying for.

I felt the flames of God's love permeating my soul. It was painful—more painful than any pain I had experienced in my life. But I knew it was necessary and would make me better. The peace of knowing I would go to heaven could not be taken from me. It undergirded me, making all the discomfort tolerable.

I thought about the wonder and wisdom of this place. God was so merciful yet also just. I was in awe of his wisdom. Praise poured forth from me. I wasn't with him yet, but I now knew that time was certain to come.

CHAPTER 35

GRIEF

> To everything there is a season, and a time to every
> purpose under the heaven. A time to weep and a time to
> laugh; a time to mourn and a time to dance.
> —Ecclesiastes 3:1,4 (KJV)

Back on the earth, the minutes turned into hours and the hours turned
into days.

Julie had fought hard not to slip deeper into the dark abyss of
depression, but she seemed unable to resist any longer. Now she was alone
looking after a disabled son and struggling to deal with the harsh realities
of being a widow.

"I can't do it," she said to Naomi as they talked on the phone. "I'm
overwhelmed. There's just too much. The dishes keep piling up, the bills
keep coming in and your brother needs help, but all I feel like doing is
staying in bed."

Naomi was silent for a moment. "I'll help you, Mom. I'll come over
this afternoon and take Stephen for the rest of the day. And I'll help you
straighten things up."

She didn't really know what else to say. Her mom had had these bouts
of depression for as long as she could remember, but never to this degree.

"And that Ron keeps calling about that business. I just can't deal with
that right now. It's too much." She silently sobbed through the phone.

"I'll be right over, Mom. Don't worry. It will be all right."

My wife hung up. Intense sadness enveloped her. She didn't want to deal with this. She didn't want to go on. It all seemed so pointless and unreal. Now thoughts of suicide became more intense, and in her mind, a real option. *Maybe that's the only way out of this. Everyone would be better off.* She didn't want to be a burden. She thought about how she would do it.

As she deliberated, the doorbell rang. She ignored it. A couple of minutes passed. Then her phone rang. It was Naomi. She was at the front door.

"I'm here, Mom. Please let me in."

She sat frozen for several moments. She just wanted to be left alone. She heard knocking and the doorbell ringing. She wanted to tell her to go away. She just wanted to end it and stop the pain.

"Mom! Mom!" she heard her daughter calling, more frantically each time.

The worry in Naomi's voice struck at her emotions. She felt the love and concern her daughter had for her. Slowly she willed herself out of bed and down the stairs. The thoughts of self harm were cast aside—at least for now.

⌀

Benny was also struggling. He was broke. He had spent the last of his money on beer and marijuana and had drunk and smoked himself numb. In the past he would always call his dad, who would send him money. But that wasn't an option now. He had tried to contact his mom, but she wasn't responding to his calls or texts. He had tried his sister, but she had said that she was all out of money as well. Anger welled up within him.

"If you're real, God, then why did you let this happen?" he yelled at the ceiling. "Everyone is suffering, and you could have stopped it. Why should I believe in you? Tell me why!"

No answer came. The silence was deafening. He slouched back onto the couch. The smell of booze and cannabis filled the air. He was mad—mad at the world, mad at himself and mad at God, if he even existed.

There was no rhyme or reason to this. He picked up an empty beer can and flung it at the wall as hard as he could. He was just mad, as angry as he had ever been in his life. It just didn't make any sense.

⌀

Keith was still in a state of disbelief. He just could not bring himself to believe what had happened. It couldn't be. How could his dad be gone? He thought about all the times he had spent with his dad. How could they be over?

"I'm going out to smoke," he told his girlfriend.

"I'll come with you."

Once outside he lit up. Two teenage boys that he didn't recognize stared at his girlfriend and laughed between themselves.

Rage built within him. "I'm going to beat their heads in," he told his girlfriend as he reached for the baton that he kept in his backpack.

"No! Don't!" she said. "It's OK."

"It's not OK!" he shot back. "It's never OK. It's never going to be OK!"

Tears rolled down his cheeks. He marched over to the boys. "Stop looking at my girlfriend or I'm going to beat your faces in!" he said and then added some profanity as he raised his baton.

They yelled at him, and one put his hand in his jacket to retrieve a knife.

Then, suddenly, a big black dog ran by. It looked exactly like his dad's black dog.

Keith turned and looked at it. "Hey, boy, is that you?" he called after the dog as it ran away from him.

The dog turned and looked at him. It was identical to his dad's. Keith ran after it and tried to follow it, but he couldn't catch it. The dog ran around a building, and by the time Keith got there it had disappeared. He searched for a while but could not find it.

His girlfriend caught up to him.

"That was my dad's dog!" he exclaimed. "I know it was him. I would know him anywhere."

She stared at him blankly. "How could that be? Your dad lived more than an hour away. What would his dog be doing here? Maybe it was a dog that just looked like him."

"I know it was him! I know it!" he replied emphatically.

Seeing the dog had reminded him of his dad. He and his dad had spent many enjoyable hours with his dog. His dad was here. He was still looking out for him. It was going to be OK. His dad was not gone after all.

Naomi left her mom's house late in the evening. She was exhausted. Her mom was in a lot of distress, and she'd had to provide a great deal of emotional as well as physical support for her. She also had to spend a lot of time with Stephen, and he had not been in a particularly good mood.

"I need sleep," she told her husband when she arrived home. "I've never seen Mom like this before. She's really, really depressed, I'm worried about her. I need to go over there every day."

She headed off to bed after giving her husband a quick kiss. She knew life would never be as it was before. But she knew she needed to keep going. That's what her dad would have wanted. That's what he would have done. And that's what she needed to do.

So grief worked its way through the hearts and souls of all those affected by my death. Each was touched in their own unique way. None was spared. Some suffered more than others, some less. Some accepted the situation, others did not. But the grief and suffering touched all; it was just a matter to what degree.

C H A P T E R   3 6

THE QUEEN

And I saw a woman clothed with the sun, with the moon
beneath her feet, and a crown of twelve stars on her head.
—Revelation 12:1 (NLT)

The grieving and suffering continued in purgatory, but it was a different sort. It was a grief of sorrow and remorse for the sinful aspects that remained on my soul. It was a grief for the way I had lived my life at times when I was in the flesh coupled with a desire to be better. It was not like the grief I had experienced when my parents died. Here I felt sorrow and remorse, but I knew it would not last. The end of it would come. But when it would come I did not know.

I discovered from others that some here had been told they were destined to stay here until the end of the world. That added to my pain. I had not been told that, but the thought of it caused me to cringe. I hoped I wasn't in that category.

I did not know how long I was in the circle of longsuffering. Time seemed to have no context here. Day and night did not exist. Slowly the flames melted away my impatience to the point that I no longer cared. I was in pain, sometimes horribly so, but the underlying peace in my soul never left me.

And then it occurred. I was told that I no longer needed to be in this circle and that I would be moving to the next one. The news came to me with calmness. My impatience was gone. I didn't make some remark about how long it had taken or been frustrated in any way. My only feeling was one of serenity.

My angel arrived to escort me. I had not seen him while I was in the circle of longsuffering. The last time I had seen him was when he had brought me here. It seemed like it had been a long while ago.

"It's nice to see you again," I said.

"It's nice to see you as well. Congratulations on moving to the next circle. How do you feel?"

"I feel a sense of peace. The feeling of always being in a hurry and intolerant of the slow speed of things has left me."

"You look better. It shows in your face that you are more at peace."

Others had told me the same thing. They said I continually looked younger and brighter. It was really noticeable here. As the stains on the inner self were burned away, the beauty of the outward self was manifested more and more. It was glorious—almost like watching a flower come into full bloom.

"You might be wondering why I did not visit you until now," my angel said. "It was because you were in the circle of longsuffering, and my not coming helped you complete the circle faster."

That made sense. "I understand. Thank you."

As of yet no one on the earth had prayed for me since my life review was completed. Also, no one had prayed for me to pray for them.

"How is my family?" I asked as we approached the next circle, the circle of remorsefulness.

"They are having difficulty dealing with their grief," he said. "Most of them miss you very much. Your youngest son has struggled greatly with just accepting that it really happened. His guardian angel transformed into a likeness of your dog in order to calm him down and keep him from a dangerous situation. Your wife has been talking to herself about suicide. She has fallen into a deep depression. She has stopped eating regularly and hardly ever leaves the house. She sleeps most of the day. She really misses you. Your respite worker and daughter have been helping out a lot with Stephen, but it is becoming a burden on them as well."

This was distressing to hear. I hated that I had left Julie when I did. I had not left my affairs in order in the event of my death and now she was suffering the consequences.

"Stephen also misses you. Lately he has become more and more difficult to look after."

I so wanted to help them in some way. I wanted to visit them. It was heart-wrenching to hear these things and not be able to help.

"Is there any way I can go see them?" I asked. "I have heard from others here that some are able to do that."

Before he could answer, we arrived at the circle of remorsefulness. A crowd had gathered. I was pretty sure it wasn't to welcome me. I didn't know what was going on.

And then I saw her. She was the most beautiful lady I had ever seen. It was not beauty in a sensual sense, although she was attractive in that way as well. It was the overall appearance of purity, love and peace that came from her. She wore a dress of pure white with a blue cloak gently lying over her shoulders and arms. She had a white veil over her head below a crown of stars and her face radiated deep affection for the souls here.

"Who is that?" I asked my angel as I looked at her with awe.

"That is Mary, Jesus's mother," he said. "She often visits the souls here, offering them comfort and kindness and reassuring them that they will be in heaven with her and her Son in due time."

I was flabbergasted. Of course I'd heard of Mary, but I had never really given her much thought. To me she was just a peasant girl who had given birth to Jesus. Seeing her now was outside anything I could have envisioned. She was astonishing. She was pure, lovely, peaceful and humble. She expressed much love for the souls she interacted with. I was not close enough to speak or interact with her, but I heard some of the words that she spoke. They were filled with comfort and consolation.

My angel spoke. "You asked me a question as we arrived here. The answer is yes that it is possible that you might be granted permission to visit your wife. But you have to request it first. And the person you need to ask is her," he said, nodding at Mary.

That surprised me even more. She was so amazing. I didn't know if I would be able to do it. I felt a sense of trepidation. She began to rise into the sky as if to leave. Then she began to move toward me. I was frozen. I stared, my mouth agape, fixated on her splendour. She passed very closely directly over me and looked into my eyes and smiled. And then she was gone.

My angel standing beside me viewed the entire thing. "I think that means she wants you to ask her."

I was astonished. I didn't know what to say.

"She'll be back," he said. "She comes here often. You can ask her then."

I only hoped I would have the courage.

My angel stayed with me for what seemed like a long while afterward going into detail about all of my family and friends. And then he left.

The flames of God's love began to burn away my lack of remorse for the things I had done during my life. I prayed more fervently for those I had harmed or caused injury to because of it. The pain I felt was extreme. But after what I had just experienced, I barely noticed.

CHAPTER 37

THE APPEARANCE

Do not neglect to show hospitality to strangers, for thereby some have entertained angels unawares.
—Hebrews 13:2 (ESV)

I wasn't in the circle or remorsefulness for long before I saw someone coming toward me. He began to run and so did I. It was my dad.

"How are you!" I said as we embraced.

"I'm very well," he said. "How are you?"

"I'm better now. I didn't expect to see you again so soon."

"I was released from the circle of contriteness and sent here. We'll be together for a while."

That warmed my heart. To have my dad with me for a while would make enduring the pain a lot easier. He was not the type to spend a lot of time with us when we were kids, so it would be nice to be with him here.

"Mary visited," he continued. "I asked her if I could visit you and she asked for permission for me. It was granted,"

He was much brighter than when I had last seen him. He also appeared younger—almost as young as me. That felt strange.

"That's fantastic. I saw her as well when I arrived here. I was stunned at the majesty of her. I was too scared to say anything to her though."

He listened intently. "Yes, I was too at first, especially considering how badly I had treated your mom during my life. I felt unworthy to speak to a woman of such beauty and purity. But after many visits I finally spoke with her. Actually, she spoke to me first. She's as kind as she is beautiful. I've spoken with her several times since."

That my dad had actually spoken to that heavenly lady several times amazed me. "You mean you know her on a first-name basis?" I asked incredulously.

"Well, I guess you could say that." He laughed.

I told him about Julie's depression and how I had asked my angel if I could visit her. "My angel said to ask Mary the next time she visits if I could gain permission to visit her. I would really like to see her and see if I could help her in anyway. What do you think?"

He thought for a moment. "I know of others who have. It's not always allowed, but it's worth a try."

"Well, I'll do it then."

After that we talked and talked. We talked about our experiences here and our lives on the earth. The flames of remorsefulness burned away, but as we talked, I hardly noticed. We laughed and cried and prayed together, thanking God that he allowed us to be here together. We talked about the things we felt remorse for now but hadn't felt during our lifetimes. And we thanked Mary for her generous kindness.

We had never had the closeness we now experienced during our time together on the earth. There was a bond of love between us that had never really existed. It was a deeper, tighter bond than anything I had ever known in the flesh.

"If I'm here when she visits next, I'll be with you," my dad said. "We'll ask together."

I was comforted by that. We parted for a while to privately contemplate and pray and praise God. And we suffered, for that was the purpose of this place—painful suffering underlaid with extreme joy and happiness. The pain here was greater than any I had ever experienced, but so was the joy. It was a combination that I could never have imagined was possible, yet it was.

⁓

My dad and my angel were right about Mary. She came again in what seemed like a very short time. This time I was close to her as she descended among us, almost close enough to touch her. But I dared not.

She was majestic, like a queen descending from her throne. Mighty angels accompanied her, beautiful yet obviously powerful. She almost glowed in a surreal fashion, yet she was completely whole. She was real. She was no ghost.

My dad stood beside me in the crowd of souls. All eyes were fixated on her. After speaking to a few others, she turned to us.

My dad spoke. "Thank you, my Lady, for allowing me to see my son and allowing me to come to this circle and be with him for a while. I deeply appreciate it." He bowed as he said it.

"It was not me who granted your request," she replied, "but my Son. Thank him."

"I will, my Lady," he said. He slowly straightened up and looked into her eyes. They were glistening. "My Lady, my son has a request for you."

She looked at me.

I started to speak but was dumbstruck. My dad gave me a nudge.

I spoke, "My wife is suffering terribly from depression since my death, my Lady. I was told by my angel that she is even considering suicide. I have heard that some here are granted permission to visit their loved ones on the earth. My angel told me I must ask you if I could be allowed to visit her and possibly comfort her."

She looked at me with tender affection. "I will ask my Son," she said. "It is he who grants permission for such requests."

She stayed and talked to everyone there and then ascended back up into the sky. I was awestruck by her. *I will never tire of her,* I thought, as my dad and I prayed together. We thanked Jesus for allowing us to be together and asked that he would bless those we had left behind on the earth.

After a brief while, my angel appeared again. He seemed happy and smiled as he greeted me. "I was just given instructions. Your request has been granted. I am to accompany you back to visit your wife."

Joy overtook me. "Oh, that's wonderful!" I said as I jumped up and hugged him. "Praise the Lord! Thank you, Jesus! Thank you, Mary!" I looked at him. "When do we go?"

"Now."

I guessed that in this place there is no time like the present since it always is the present. So we left.

We flew out of the place of purification and into space back to the earth.

My angel explained as we went. "You have been given permission to appear to her for a moment and speak a few words to her. That is a rare permission—not often granted. You may tell her where you are, and you may ask her to pray for you. You may tell her you are praying for her, but that is all. You may not touch her."

I thought about that for a moment. "May I ask her to pray for my dad also?"

"That would be allowed."

"I would love to appear to her, but I don't want to frighten her badly. I remember her telling me a story about her mom when she was young and how her mom's grandmother appeared to her after she had died. It scared her badly. I used to not really believe that story, but I do now. I don't want to scare her."

My angel thought about that for a moment. He seemed to be losing patience with me.

"All right. I can help with that. I will speak to her first to prepare her for seeing you. I will disguise myself as a human so that she does not know it is me. Then when you appear to her, it will not be as much of a surprise. It will also prove beyond all doubt that she was not hallucinating or dreaming when she sees you."

That sounded like a good plan to me. We entered the earth's atmosphere. Again, I marvelled at its great beauty. It seemed that everything God created was marked by beauty and love and purpose.

"You can watch while I speak with her," my angel said. "But do not appear to her until the next day. We must give her time to mull over what I say to her. While we wait, you may visit your other family members and friends, but you are not allowed to appear to them or make contact with them in any way. Permission for that has only been granted for your wife."

"That will be all right," I said. "Thank you."

We arrived at our house. It looked the same as it did the day I died. My wife was still in her nightgown in the kitchen. I longed to hug and kiss her. She seemed so lonely, so down. But I was not allowed. We went back outside.

My angel surveyed the surroundings. No one was around. He then morphed into a human. He looked like a delivery man. He had a small box in his hands. I was astonished at his transformation.

He went to the front door and rang the doorbell. It took a while, but after a few moments Julie answered. She was dishevelled, which was so unlike her. She had always been careful to keep her appearance looking good.

"I have a package for you," he said, handing it to her.

"Thank you," she replied without her usual smile.

"You don't seem so happy," he said.

She looked at him a moment, a frown on her face. "I'm not. My husband was killed in an accident recently. I really miss him. Now I'm alone with my disabled son, and he is difficult to deal with. I no longer have my husband to help me."

Her words were hard for me to hear. How I wished I could morph back into my body and help her.

My angel paused. "He may still be able to help you," he said. "Just ask him."

She seemed a bit startled by his response. "Well, I know he's in heaven now, but I don't know how he can help me. How can I ask him to help me?"

"Tomorrow you can ask him," my angel said. "Do it then." He turned and left.

My wife stood at the door puzzled by his reply. She watched him leave. "Where is your vehicle?"

"I walked," he called back.

She shook her head, bewildered by this odd deliveryman. She closed the door. My angel again surveyed the surroundings, and seeing no one, transformed back into his angelic form.

My wife opened the door again and looked out. The deliveryman was gone. She went to the end of the driveway. He was nowhere to be seen. Mystified, she went inside and opened the package. In it was a necklace of beads with a cross attached. She took it out and looked at it. She took a picture of it and sent it to our daughter. Then she phoned her and told her about the encounter she had just had with the strange deliveryman and what he had said.

"I think that's called a rosary," Naomi told her. "One of my friends showed me hers once. I think you pray the prayer and then you can talk to people in heaven or something like that. That's probably what he meant. He probably heard about what happened and is trying to cheer you up."

"I never ordered this," my wife said. "I think he just made a mistake. He was so weird."

I stayed and listened to them talk. It was so nice to hear their voices again.

That evening my wife went to her computer and researched rosary beads and the prayers associated with them. She pondered what she learned and the events of the day. Then she went to bed and slept better than she had in days.

I visited my other children and friends while she was sleeping. It was so good to see them again even though most of them were in bed. This time I also saw their guardian angels watching over them. My angel spoke with each one. They all seemed to know each other well. That would make sense, I thought, as they would see each other a lot being connected to family members as they were.

The next day we were back at our house. My wife was in bed.

"Now is the time," my angel said. "Focus all your energy on appearing and speaking and she will be able to see and hear you. Then speak the words to her you wish to say. Be brief."

I went to the foot of the bed. She was so beautiful as she roused from sleep. Her hair stuck out in all directions, just as I remembered. She reached for a book on her nightstand.

I focused all of my energy as my angel had instructed. And then I appeared.

My wife was stunned. She almost jumped off of the bed. She pulled her blanket up to the level of her eyes.

I spoke. "I am in purgatory. Pray for me," I said, "and for my dad."

She looked at me for a few seconds. Then she said, "Help me. I feel so alone and depressed. Pray for me."

"I will," I promised, and I disappeared.

"Well done," my angel said. "Now you must go back to the place of purification."

We flew back. I only hoped that my wife knew it was really me.

"Do you think she understood?" I asked my angel.

"She understood," he replied, "and she will never forget that moment for as long as she lives."

As we entered purgatory, the flames of remorsefulness began burning my stains and blemishes away again. The pain now became intense. I wished I had been more remorseful for the bad things I had done in my life.

But the pain was mitigated by my thoughts about those I had just visited. I would wait to see if there was any response.

CHAPTER 38

THE PRAYERS

*It is therefore a holy and wholesome thought to pray for
the dead, that they may be loosed from sins.*
—2 Maccabees 12:46 (CLB)

My wife sat stunned, the covers pulled up to her face. Had she really just
seen and heard what she thought she'd just seen and heard? She had talked
to her husband, and he had answered. It could not have been a dream
because she was wide awake. It could not have been a hallucination because
she was not ill or on any drugs.

Then she remembered the strange deliveryman from the day before.
It was odd that he had said that I could ask my husband today for help.
How did he know that? And why did he give me that rosary? It was all too
much to just be a coincidence.

She picked up her phone and called Naomi. She told her that she had
just seen me and that she had even talked with me.

My daughter was beside herself. "Oh, wow, Mom. That's unbelievable!
He really appeared at the foot of your bed? He really is all right! See, I told
you that rosary had something to do with praying to people in heaven."

My wife was silent for a moment. "Yes, you did. The thing is, he didn't
say he was in heaven. He said he was in purgatory. And he asked me to
pray for him. And apparently Grandpa is there too."

My daughter did not respond immediately. "I've heard of purgatory,"
she finally said. "Isn't that some kind of Catholic thing? But we aren't
Catholic."

"Well, whether we are or not, that's where he said he is, and he asked me to pray for him and Grandpa."

They talked for a long while about the turn of events. They talked about the strange deliveryman and the things he had said and done and how he didn't even have a vehicle.

"He might have been an angel," my daughter said.

My wife hadn't considered that. "You know, you might be right."

After the call, my wife got down on her knees. She prayed for her husband and her father-in-law. She had never prayed for the dead before. She wasn't sure if she was doing it right. But she did know one thing; it sure felt right.

She went on her computer and began researching praying for the dead. My wife had always been very good at research. She discovered a lot about the practice and the teachings of the Catholic Church on the topic. It gave her a feeling of purpose that she hadn't had in many days. In fact, it was the best she had felt since her husband's death. The depression seemed to be fading, at least for now.

⌘

In the place of purification my suffering continued. I told my dad about my visit with Julie.

He was pleased. "Thank you for telling her to pray for me. It's really making things more bearable."

After a while my angel visited me again. "I see your wife has been praying for you regularly since our visit."

"Yes, and not only her—my daughter, our respite worker, Stephen and even my uncle have prayed for me. My wife must be telling everybody about it. It feels good. It eases some of the pain."

The angel looked at me and smiled. "Well, your wife is doing more than just praying for you. She has been doing research on praying for the dead. She found out that there was a pilgrimage sight where people would be praying for people here. She obtained the details and has been asking all your children, relatives and friends if they would like to go. She has offered to pay for anyone who cannot afford it out of your life insurance money. Several have agreed to go. It looks like they will be going soon. I've been there. Mary also goes there regularly."

It was heartening to hear what my angel had to say.

"It is a beautiful thing that your wife is doing for you," he continued. "Organizing a pilgrimage to pray for you and your father will benefit both of you greatly."

I considered what he said. "You know, Julie has always been like that. She either does something big or doesn't do anything at all. That used to annoy me. But I have to say I'm happy about it now."

He laughed. Then he said something that really surprised me. "You may not be here much longer. I'll probably see you again soon."

I wasn't sure what to say. "Thank you for your patience and helping me during my visit to my wife."

"You're welcome," he said, and then he departed.

The prayers continued to come for my dad and me. After what seemed like a short time, I was told I would be moving to another circle. I said goodbye to my dad for a while as he was still not finished in the circle of remorsefulness.

"Just don't forget to see me before you go to heaven," he said as we embraced.

"If I do, I certainly will," I replied.

His pain had been lessened by the prayers for him. He continued looking better and better.

True to his word, my angel came to escort me to my next circle on a different level—the circle of temperance. The flames continued to burn, but they seemed to be less and less. It seemed that with every prayer offered on my behalf, my pain subsided and the stains on my soul dropped away.

CHAPTER 39

THE PILGRIMAGE

Blessed are those whose strength is in you, who have set
their hearts on pilgrimage.

—Psalm 84:5 (NIV)

My wife called everyone in the family to see who might be interested in going on the pilgrimage. The offer of a free trip turned out to be irresistible for some.

"Hey, if it's a free trip, I'm in," Benny said.

My uncle Ron was only too delighted to go as he was still in negotiations with Julie over the business and wanted to stay in her good graces. He thought that if he went, he might be able to negotiate a better deal.

Naomi jumped at the opportunity to get a break from the kids for a few days.

Keith saw it as an adventure and a chance to hang out with his older brother for a while.

Lindsey didn't really see the point, but she offered to give Keith extra spending money. Stephen loved going anywhere with his siblings, and his respite worker Fred agreed to come and help out.

So, although most had some form of ulterior motive attached, they all agreed to come and pray for me and my dad in purgatory.

The morning of the trip, not everyone was in a good mood. Benny and Keith quarrelled over who would sit where. Stephen didn't like sitting beside Fred. Ron was sullen and quiet.

"I don't know how this is going to work out," Julie said to Naomi.

My wife managed to get the first Mass that they went to offered for me and my dad. She had researched the topic and had learned that offering a Mass for the dead could be highly effective in helping them move on from purgatory.

As they entered the church at the pilgrimage site for the first time, my daughter was astonished.

"This is so beautiful," she said. "This is the first time I've ever been inside a Catholic church."

She felt a wave of peace come over her as she stepped into a pew. She had never experienced that before and certainly never in a church. "I feel so calm and at peace here," she told her mom as she prayed.

"I know what you mean," Julie whispered back. "It feels so good and so right here."

Benny and Keith really didn't want to go into the church. They would much rather have just hung out outside and smoked. But my wife persuaded them to go in. They grudgingly acquiesced. They sat together at the back. That was a seating arrangement they could both agree on. Church was not their thing and certainly not praying in church. But as they observed everyone else praying, they both felt it was only right that they pray for their dad and grandfather as well. So they did. The quiet and solemnity of the place infiltrated them.

"I don't really believe in all this stuff, but I do feel calm here," Benny said to Keith. "It's almost as good as a joint. Well, not quite." He grinned.

Fred sat beside Stephen, who was eager to pray for his dad and grandpa.

"My mom said we can help my dad and grandpa get to heaven if we pray for them here. So that's what I'm going to do, you know."

"That's good," Fred replied. "I will pray for them as well."

Although Fred was a believer and had been all his life, he really didn't believe much in praying for the dead. Sure, he sometimes uttered a prayer for someone after he heard about their death, but that was about all. He figured it wasn't going to hurt anything if he did it here though.

The next evening they went to the cemetery as it was a special day to pray for the dead. The gravestones were all covered with flowers, candles and pictures of the departed. The glowing candles in the darkness gave forth an eerie beauty. My wife had found out that special indulgences could be obtained for those in purgatory if they prayed there in conjunction with attending Mass and a few other things.

My uncle's heart was moved by the scene. As he prayed by a tombstone, he felt true remorse for some of his actions in his life. A transformation of sorts seemed to come over him. Experiencing this was causing him to think about what was really important in life. He had feelings he had never felt before.

Later, as they walked back to the hotel, he uttered words he had never uttered before, or ever thought he would utter. "I will pay you whatever amount you want for Johnny's share in the business if you want to sell it," he said to Julie. "I'm truly sorry for the way I treated him. I know he would have wanted you to be looked after."

Julie looked at him with a face of gratitude and forgiveness. She gave Ron a hug, tears falling down her cheeks.

As they journeyed home, the group seemed to have coalesced into a unified, happy travelling assemblage. They were all getting along better than they ever had before. All had been on their best behaviour. Neither Benny or Keith had smoked or drank for the entire trip.

"It's a minor miracle," my wife said about the changes she'd seen.

Perhaps, however, the biggest change had occurred within her. The depression that had so tightly gripped her had now vanished. The suicidal thoughts were gone. She felt a new purpose in her life. She was determined that she would now care for Stephen to the best of her abilities and be the best version of herself for however many days she had left. She now knew with certainty what lay beyond death.

Even though Lindsey did not go on the trip she too was affected. Upon returning home, she noticed a change in Keith. He was different somehow—he seemed more mature and in control of his emotions. Her unbelief began to teeter, if only a little.

Faith had grown on the trip, and where there was none, seeds had been planted. It had been a truly rich experience for all, much more so than any had expected.

C H A P T E R   4 0

COMPLETION

And let endurance have its perfect result, so that you may
be perfect and complete, lacking in nothing.
—James 1:4 (NASB)

My angel visited me and related the events from the pilgrimage. He told
me about the changes that had occurred to everyone who had gone, even
to Lindsey.

Jesus's words came to my mind.

"I see now that if I had not died and they had not gone on that
pilgrimage, those changes would not likely have occurred. Maybe that's
what Jesus meant when he said they would benefit more from my leaving
than if I stayed."

My angel nodded. "That could certainly be part of it."

He stayed and filled me in on other details about my family and
friends.

"I will see you again soon," he said as he departed.

Time passed, or at least what seemed like time, if it even existed in
this place. The suffering continued, but it seemed to diminish quickly,
almost to the point that I hardly noticed it anymore. The pilgrimage had
had a huge effect. The prayers and Mass resulted almost immediately in
a reduction in my pain and a removal of blemishes on my soul. Those I
had tried to help during my life now in turn helped me. I marvelled at

the beauty of the reciprocities in life. It seemed that as I helped others, I received help in return. And now I knew that even extended until after my death.

The purification of my soul seemed to greatly speed up now. The prayers from the earth continued to come. I prayed fervently for all those I had left behind and those I had harmed while I was alive. I prayed they would be able to make the changes they needed during their earthly lives so they would not have to come to this place after death, or at least not for long.

I moved quickly from circle to circle and level to level. I felt the stains on my soul decreasing along with the suffering. I was told by others that my appearance continued to brighten and brighten as I moved upward.

And then it happened. Mary arrived in all her splendour with her angelic accompaniment. Her face radiated joy. One of her angels blew a trumpet. It seemed she was about to make an important announcement.

"Tomorrow is Christmas Day on the earth," she said. "Some of you have now completed your time here and are ready to go to heaven."

She looked directly at me. "You are one of the ones to whom I refer," she said, her face a picture of love and affection.

I melted. I melted right there on the spot. I did not expect it. I wanted to hug her. "Thank you, my Lady! Thank you so much! Thank you, Jesus! Thank you, Father, Son and Holy Spirit! If I could, I would hug you!"

"In heaven, my child," she replied. "The prayers and the pilgrimage that your wife organized all helped greatly for you to attain the removal of the stain of sin from your soul. I saw her and the others when they were there. Some asked for me to intercede for you and your dad to my Son. This I did. He has decided that you are now ready to wear the garments of heaven."

My angel appeared beside me. "Congratulations, my friend." We embraced. This time it almost felt as equals.

I felt totally whole. I felt totally complete. I felt perfect. Total love and peace exuded from me. I felt entirely clean and pure. All pain had evaporated. All worry and regret and sorrow and doubt were gone. My soul was ready to live with its Creator. I was true and without flaw. I had become who I needed to become.

I bowed to Mary, my Queen, and again thanked her for her help. She came to each of her sons and daughters individually and kissed us on the forehead as we bowed. She comforted those who still had to wait longer in the place of purification and then she left, ascending into the greyish, half-lit sky.

My angel said, "You have been granted permission to visit your wife once more before you go to heaven. After you enter there, you will not be allowed to visit the earth again during her lifetime. Do you wish to do this?"

"Oh yes, yes, I would like that very much," I said.

We returned to the earth.

We arrived in my wife's bedroom on what was Christmas Eve. She was reading as she sat up in her bed.

I focused all my energy and appeared at the foot of her bed.

Again, she was startled, but this time she did not pull her covers up to her eyes.

"Thank you," I said. "Tomorrow I am going to heaven. I will not be allowed to visit you again."

"I love you," she said, tears rolling down her cheeks.

I paused to look at her beautiful face one last time until we would meet again in heaven.

"I love you too," I said, and then I vanished.

My angel allowed me to visit my children and grandchildren one last time. I was told that I would not be allowed to visit them during their lifetimes. I could not appear to them or make contact with them. They all seemed to be doing reasonably well and adjusting to life without me. I stayed with each one for as long as I was allowed and prayed for them.

We returned to the place of purification for the last time. My journey there was almost complete. Tomorrow was Christmas Day, and I felt like a kid again waiting in eager anticipation.

CHAPTER 41

THE BEGINNING

Then the angel showed me the river of the water of life, as clear as crystal, flowing from the throne of God and of the Lamb down the middle of the great street of the city. On each side of the river stood the tree of life, bearing twelve crops of fruit, yielding it's fruit every month. And the leaves of the tree are for the healing of the nations. No longer will there be any curse. The throne of God and of the Lamb will be in the city, and his servants will serve him. They will see his face, and his name will be on their foreheads. There will be no more night. They will not need the light of a lamp or the light of the sun, for the Lord God will give them light. And they will reign forever and ever.
—Revelation 22:1–5 (NIV)

"I need to see my dad," I told my angel. "Do you know where he is? I promised I would try to see him before I went to heaven."

My angel smiled. "When Mary arrives to escort you to heaven, you will see him."

My angel took me to a plaza-like area I had not been to before. Thousands of other souls from the other circles were there as well.

"Are all of these going to heaven as well?" I asked.

"Yes," my angel said. "Christmas Day on the earth is a time when many souls go from the place of purification to heaven."

Every soul was there with their guardian angels. The excitement and anticipation was palpable.

"Hello, son. I was told you would be here."

I turned to see my dad.

"I'm going to heaven today, Dad!" I said excitedly. "I hope it won't be long before I see you again."

My dad laughed. "It won't be, son. I'm going to heaven today too."

Joy burst forth from both of us. We embraced. He looked so vibrant and robust.

"The prayers from everyone who went on the pilgrimage made a huge difference. They shortened my stay here. Thank you again for asking them to pray for me."

Trumpets sounded. Mary and her angelic host arrived.

"It is time for you all to be given the garments of heaven," she said. "You must wear them to enter there."

The angels brought out the garments. First, we put on formal white gowns, stunning in their elegance. They were whiter than anything found on the earth, and they breathed purity. Then we received beautiful golden sashes that sparkled brilliantly. We literally glowed. The garments were dazzling.

The angels then brought multicoloured robes and placed them on each of us. There were hundreds, if not thousands, of colours in them, far more than I had ever seen before. The robes were smoother than silk and the phosphorescence of them was stunning. It was like the very clothes we wore were alive.

Mary and the angels then led us out of the place of purification, and we began to fly. We soon saw a bright light in the distance; the most magnificent, blazingly white light imaginable. As we approached, it became apparent that it was a city with enormous walls around it. The walls seemed to be made of all sorts of gemstones that glittered spectacularly in the light. A huge crowd was waiting outside the walls. They too seemed really excited.

They rushed toward us as we arrived, the greatest greeting party conceivable. They were our friends and relatives who were already in heaven waiting to welcome us. My mom was the first to greet my dad and me as we rushed into her arms.

"Welcome, welcome!" she said, tears of joy streaming down her face. "Welcome home."

One by one we met those who had preceded us to this perfect place. It was the most joyous, jubilant gathering I had ever experienced. The mirth and gleeful happiness knew no bounds. After the greetings, we approached the gate. It was colossal. It appeared to be made of pearl or marble and all of one piece. It glistened a brilliant white radiance of absolute purity and sanctity.

Mary led us in, and we moved to a wide, exquisite street of what appeared to be solid gold. It had a transparency about it that sparkled. We heard music—beautiful, angelic music, not too loud and not too soft, coming from all directions. It was praising God and it perfectly accentuated the surroundings. There were many, many people here, far too many to count, all resplendent in appearance and blissfully joyful in their affect.

A breathtakingly beautiful river of crystal-clear water ran down the middle of the great street. The water was wholly pure and felt like life itself. Marvellous trees were on each side of the river bearing all manner of fruits. There were animals and people all along the way, all in perfect harmony. Brilliant flowers of every kind could be seen and they, too, seemed to be singing praises to God.

And then the brightness brightened even more. We were there. In front of me was the most awe inspiring overwhelmingly majestic sight I would ever see. I fell to my knees and began praising God.

I was at the throne of God. The Father, Son and Holy Spirit were before me. I was speechless. I saw them clearly now face to face. Thousands of angels were in the background offering praise. The river of crystal-clear water flowed from the throne. As I knelt before them it was as if I was the only one there—as if all the others had disappeared.

Mary stood beside Jesus. I saw his features clearly now for the first time. In a way he looked like the many images of him I had seen on the earth, but they were pale comparisons to the reality. I felt immersed in love. They looked directly at me and spoke to me as if I was the only person in heaven.

"Welcome, my son," the Father said. Love permeated his deep voice. "You have lived your life on the earth, where you were tried and tested.

You used the talents we gave you for the good of the kingdom of God and your fellow man. Now you will be rewarded for what you achieved for our kingdom with the abilities you were given. You will begin your new life, the true life you were created for, and you will use the rewards you are given in that new life. You have suffered much, and you have been joined with my Son in that suffering. You have been purified from the stain of sin and you are now pure and holy. Now you will live in heaven for all of eternity. Well done, my good and faithful servant."

Tears of joy rolled down my cheeks. "Thank you, Father," was all I could say.

I remained on my knees in this most solemn moment.

"Now you will receive your rewards for the things you did during your life, my son," he said.

Jesus approached and presented me with the rewards. They were beyond anything I could have ever thought possible, beyond the description of any human words. God's name was then placed on my forehead. I was completely humbled.

"Thank you, Lord," I whispered.

"Go in peace, my son," he said.

I left the throne area and re-joined my family, friends and angels. They had all witnessed the entire thing and saluted me with the most robust, heart-warming congratulations ever.

We went to a great banquet where we celebrated with jubilation and joy and festivity all transfused with unfathomable love. This was Christmas in heaven. No earthly celebration could begin to compare with it, no earthly words could possibly properly describe it. We ate and drank and danced and talked, but mostly we praised God.

I met all my relatives and friends who had preceded me here during my life and many of my ancestors who had lived before I was born. I learned more about my close family at this feast than I had learned in my entire lifetime. But I also learned that we were all related, all humans going right back to our first parents, Adam and Eve. We truly were one big human family. We laughed and rejoiced and enjoyed one another.

It went on without the constraint of time, which had no relevancy here. Fatigue, worry and feelings that I needed to be somewhere else were no more. Total energy, complete ease and exhilaration engulfed me. Not a hint of pain inflicted me, not an iota of discomfort burdened me. Pure contentment and love encompassed me.

Then a little girl approached me. I marvelled at how much she reminded me of my daughter. She had an infectious smile that radiated love.

"Can you play a game with me, Grandfather?" she asked.

I did not hesitate.

"Oh yes, my granddaughter," I said. "I can play a game with you. I have plenty of time. I have all the time in heaven."

I once read in the Bible where it said that the day of our death is better than the day of our birth. I could never understand that. How could the day that I die be better than the day I was born? But now I understood.

For I'd had many great days in my life. I'd had days of triumph and days of love, days of celebration and days of joy, days of reward and days of pleasure. I'd had days where I experienced many wonderful things and felt the full range of emotions. But I now realized that none of those days were my greatest day. I now knew that the best day of my life was the day I finally discovered who I really was. It was the day I met my Creator—the day I found out where I was going and what I had to do to get there. It was the day where everything in my life at last made sense. It was the day that I came to understand and the day that I knew I was understood.

Yes, I now knew that the very finest day of my life had been the very final one—the last day of my life.

04164408-00961357

Printed in the United States
by Baker & Taylor Publisher Services